D1525433

# On the Way Home

## Skye Warren

# On the Way Home

**Clint**

For eight months I've been deep under cover as a special operator in the Army. On the plane ride home, all I want is a hot shower and a long sleep. But a Dear John text message leaves me stranded. I need a ride and a place to stay, and the pretty stewardess is more than willing.

**Della**

It's supposed to be a simple trade—the passenger in seat 34B for my sister. But the sexy soldier is more than I can handle in all the best ways. He trusts me, but I can't save him. No one can. Sometimes trouble has a way of following you home.

*On the Way Home is a dark new adult romance intended for readers over eighteen.*

# PROLOGUE

THREE PLANTS LINED up in a row on my windowsill, framed by the butterfly curtains Caro had made. My science-fair experiment was going to test how well plants grew under harsh conditions. That meant depriving them of water, of sunlight. And I just couldn't do it. I was supposed to choose which plant would live and which one would die. It felt mean.

Now all the plants were the same size, and I had no idea how to explain that in my report.

Frowning, I tried to remember what the teacher had said, something about the difference between the result and the conclusion. I bit my lip. This was important. I'd told my teacher I wanted to be a nurse, and she hadn't laughed. She said I better learn science if I was going to be a nurse, so I wanted to get this right.

A crash came from outside, and the pencil fell out of my hand, clattering on the desk.

Caro had been painting her nails purple, but now she stopped halfway through. She put a finger to her mouth. *Shhh.* She pressed against the door, trying to listen to the conversation. She always got to listen, and I had to do my homework. I wanted to hear too.

More shouts came, but they were too muffled to understand. Georgia was out there, with the grownups. Ever since she had turned seventeen and started her secret job at night, she got to be out there when they were fighting. Georgia got to be in the living room and Caro got to listen at the door, but I was supposed to finish my science report. It wasn't fair.

The sound of someone getting slapped made me wince.

"I'm going out there," Caro said. Her face was as serious as I'd ever seen her. She didn't even look as scared as I felt. "Whatever happens, don't come out, okay?"

I nodded quickly. My stomach felt like it was tearing itself up inside. Besides, I didn't want to go out there anymore. Shouting was okay, but hitting hurt. A lot.

Caro stepped forward and gripped both sides of my face. It made me tense even though I knew she'd never hurt me. Her gaze was steady on mine, clear as a sunny day. "I'm serious. When I walk outta this room, you lock the door behind me. No matter what you hear, you don't come out. Promise me that."

I swallowed. "Okay. I promise."

She stood by the door another second. It got all quiet outside, the silence so loud I could hear it buzzing in my ears. Then she slipped into the dark hallway. I followed her to the door and turned the lock inside the knob. I knew it wouldn't really hold someone back, but usually no one came to our room. My heart thudded in my chest. I could feel its beat all the way out to my fingers and toes, like the way your whole body thumps when a car with loud music rolls by.

Caro wasn't here to stop me anymore, so I pressed my ear to the door. Couldn't hear anything, though. Maybe she had calmed everyone down. She did that for me too, holding me at night if I had bad dreams.

There was a voice again, but it wasn't shouting. Low, like from a man. Papa? Or the person who came to visit us? A door slammed. Maybe he was gone. We'd be okay again, I was sure of it. At least until he came back.

I opened the door to see. A shot rang out, so loud in my ears, like an explosion. It made me go cold and still. Frozen. I'd never heard a sound like that so close, never inside our house. Only sometimes I heard it far away, from another street, while Caro would rock me in bed. Then the sirens would come.

It was the sound of a gun.

"Caro," I shouted, running into the living room.

At first all I could see was chaos, like how you spin and spin and then throw up. Everything was blurry. There were men here, lots of them. Papa was here and men wearing suits. I didn't care about them. But then I saw Caro. She was okay! Relief let me breathe again.

She was leaning over something, kneeling on the ground. Thick brown hair was spread all around. I'd seen that hair brushed and brushed. Georgia had such pretty hair. Dark red liquid was matting the strands, pressing it close to her head like clay.

I stepped forward. "Caro?"

3

She only cried harder, and I knew. I felt pain, harder than any slap I'd ever gotten. "Georgia?" I whispered.

My oldest sister didn't move. She lay on the floor with her eyes closed and Caro crying over her. I stood on the other side of the room, but it felt even farther away. On the other side of the planet.

All I heard was the shot, so loud, ringing in my head like a bell. One man stepped right in front of me. He was smiling as if he'd just found something great, but I didn't trust that smile. I didn't like it.

He bent down on one knee, at eye level. "What's your name?" he asked.

*Caro! Georgia!* I wanted to run to them. I should be with my sisters, but I couldn't move. Especially when the man put his fingers under my chin. His eyes were cold and gray, like silver. His mouth moved, and I saw him speak more than heard him.

"I know your mother's preference for geography," he murmured. "Georgia. Carolina. So what's your name, little one? Texas? Montana?" When I didn't answer, he laughed. "It's okay. You'll tell me eventually."

The ringing cleared from my head, leaving only my teacher's voice. *Results are what happened. The conclusion is what it means.* I knew then that my sister Georgia was dead. And it meant nothing would be okay ever again.

# CHAPTER ONE
## CLINT

I COULD BE comfortable strapped into a Chinook, with full body armor and another hundred fifty pounds of equipment on top of that. I could HALO down to a cross-fire insertion, no problem. But flying coach on a standard commercial airline was killer.

Everything seemed tiny, as if I'd walked onto a display version of a real airplane. Due to the design of the plane, the rows on this side only had two seats. My buddy James had taken the window seat, but the aisle didn't give me room to stretch. My legs were folded like a pretzel to fit into the small amount of legroom. My head cleared the headrest by almost a foot. My body jutted into the aisle, but there was nothing to do about that without pushing into James beside me.

The pretty stewardess walked by, her hip brushing my shoulder.

"I'm sorry," she murmured.

*Della,* her name tag read. She was slender and careful, but that didn't matter when I was taking up half the aisle with my shoulder.

"My fault," I managed to say. It came out more like a

rumble.

The lightest whisper of cloth, her blue uniform against my fatigues. A wisp of heat and a faint smell of peaches. It was too much. As if I were goddamned Sleeping Beauty, my dick woke the hell up.

She smiled then, and it was way too late to pretend I wasn't getting hot at the sight of her.

Jesus, those lips. And the little upturned smile, the one that said she knew exactly what I was thinking.

Well, maybe not exactly. No way were her thoughts as desperate as mine. Eight months away from the States had taken its toll, with not even enough time or energy to beat off with regularity.

No privacy, either, but then we didn't care about that. You couldn't be fastidious in a godforsaken jungle. They send a bunch of eighteen-year-old testosterone junkies into the wild, what else is gonna happen? There'd been a time we'd all go into a firefight, walk out with no bullet holes, then head back to our bunks and jack off like we were synchronized swimming.

Not this time, though.

After our first two tours in Afghanistan, James and I got picked up to work as part of a joint task force. Guess we impressed somebody. We couldn't even drink back then—at least, not legally—but we were handed some of the most lethal weapons and secretive recording equipment in use.

Since then we had continued to fight, but not on any sanctioned battlefield. Our ops were secretive and lethal and mostly not even acknowledged by the US government. We lived and worked in the darkest parts of the world, then came home on leave so we could remember why we did it.

My twenty-third birthday had come and gone, spent with some of the most disgusting human beings I'd ever met and had to pretend like I was their new best friend. I shuddered just remembering some of the things I'd witnessed, unable to do anything without blowing my cover. I'd seen some bad shit in my life, but nothing compared to those sights. When I closed my eyes, I could still see those young girls. Way too young. I wanted to wash myself off just for being around that, even if we had taken it down in the end.

Mission accomplished. Go home.

So it was a real fucking surprise when my body was suddenly interested in the sweet-smelling, hot-as-hell stewardess.

"Can I get you something?" she asked. "Water? A soda?"

Suddenly my mouth was dry. "No, thanks."

She smiled again. God, she really needed to stop that. "I think I can rustle up some pretzels if you ask nicely?"

Nope, wasn't doing that.

"I could use some pretzels," James said from beside me.

Really? "Nah, we're good. Don't worry about us."

"All right. You boys let me know." She sauntered off, leaving both James and I staring. Man, that skirt hugged her so nicely…

"What the hell was that for?" James said. "She would've come back."

"And then what, asshole? You've got Rachel."

"And you've got… what's her name? Chelsea."

"Yeah," I lied. I'd been lying for a few weeks now, ever since I'd landed at the base in Germany where I could check my messages. *Dear Clint, I'm sorry to tell you like this but…* A Dear John text message. A remote control breakup. It had happened to enough of our friends that I knew what the reaction would be if I told people. Pity, from the guys who could still look at me. Avoidance from everyone else, as if the condition of being dumped was contagious.

So I hadn't told anyone, not even James. And hell, maybe it wouldn't be that bad. Me and Chels had a good thing going. Maybe not good, but it wasn't bad either. And separation was always hard. For all I knew, we'd patch things up right away and then I'd be glad I never told James, who would've given her a hard time after that.

She was probably going to pick me up at the airport, just like we'd planned, and here I was checking out another woman. The eight months had done a number on both of us, that was all. We'd work it out.

I glanced down the aisle at the stewardess—*Della*—who had bent to speak to another passenger. "The point is, she's doing her job. She doesn't need us bothering her."

"Hey, you were the one groping her."

"With my shoulder?"

"And flirting," James added.

"I was not flirting." I would have known if I'd been flirting, right? And I definitely hadn't done that. She was working. The last thing she needed was two horndogs using up her time or ogling her. "And stop looking."

"That's your argument? There's nothing wrong with looking, man. It's harmless. You think when our girls are back home, they don't look?"

I did not like where this conversation was going. One of the main reasons to send a Dear John letter, as opposed to waiting until I got back, was for another guy. It pinched something in my chest to imagine Chelsea moving on that quick. I turned my irritation on my best friend. "Do you actually hear yourself talk?"

"I stand by my assertion. I don't care if Rachel checks out some hot doctor at her hospital. Long as she saves up the horniness for when I get back."

"Yeah, okay. You write that on your anniversary card."

"Shit, it's my anniversary?"

"Hell if I know."

We were quiet a moment. James was probably working out the dates in his head, trying to figure out if he needed to pick up a present from the airport gift shop. Me? I pretended to be asleep. Shut my eyes, even when the stewardess came back this way. But I could still see her long legs and black heels, and I had to admit: I was peeking. I couldn't help it. There was something about her... the way she moved... so alluring...

"She walks like a stripper," James muttered when she'd passed us by.

My eyes snapped open. "I am seriously going to punch you in the face right now."

"What? I didn't mean it in a bad way. It's a good walk. A good, professional walk."

"Your nose will be broken, and then you'll have to explain to Rachel why it's broken."

"Okay, I'll stop. But only because Rachel would freak out. She worries about me."

James said the last part carelessly, but I still felt it like a blow, as if he'd beat me without even trying. Rachel *did* worry about him. A lot. It was a point of contention between them, but also a sign of how much they cared about each other.

Had Chelsea worried about me while I was gone? Hardly.

"Hey..." I cleared my throat. "How do you and Rachel reconnect when you get back home?"

"You really want me to answer that question?"

"Besides sex."

"What else is there?"

"Nice. I mean... hell, I don't know. The emotional connection."

James narrowed his eyes in suspicion. "Are we secretly on *Oprah?* Look, man. The emotional connection is the easy part. You like a girl, you spend time with her, you get closer. That's the connection. And the sex doesn't hurt. Well, unless you want it to."

"Ha-ha," I said, but unease speared through me. It sounded so simple when James spelled it out. You like a girl, spend time with her. I'd had that with Chelsea once, hadn't I?

I couldn't remember.

Leaning over, I looked forward and back. The aisles were clear. No sign of Della or any other flight attendant. Frustrated for reasons I couldn't explain, I settled into my seat—as well as I could—and closed my eyes. One thing you learned in the army was how to sleep, even if you were uncomfortable, anytime, anyplace.

Not this time, apparently. But I kept my eyes shut and pretended.

# CHAPTER TWO
## CLINT

"**S**HIT."

The low word snapped me out of sleep. I went on high alert, my body recognizing the stress in James's voice before I was fully awake. My hand went to my back, where a handgun had been stashed for most of my time undercover, a shitty substitute for a bona fide holster. But my waistband was empty. In fact, I had no gear at all.

I was on a plane.

Wiping my face, I demanded hoarsely, "What's wrong?"

"Trouble," James murmured with a nod to the front.

The plane. We were on the plane, and the first place my mind went after *trouble* was Della. If Della was in trouble, I was going to... what? I jolted out of my seat, pushing back the people who had stuck their heads into the aisle to see better.

There was Della, kneeling in the aisle, holding someone's head in her lap.

"Back up," I snapped to the man who was leaning over Della's shoulder for a better look. He'd been sitting beside the woman who was currently on the ground, but he was of no use.

After handling many medical emergency situations in the military, two things were clear to me immediately: one, the older woman was in anaphylactic shock, and two, Della was an asset. Worry filled her eyes, but she was calm and breathing steady. No panic, though the same couldn't be said for some of the people around us. I heard James behind me, clearing the seats nearby to give us room.

Della looked at me. "She has a medical exception for her EpiPen."

That's right. Needles wouldn't be allowed except in extreme cases. As the stewardess, she would know about them. "Do you know where she keeps it?"

"It's not in her pockets. I already checked."

That was the most common place to store it for easy access. A quick search of the purse didn't reveal anything. Shit. Even kneeling on the seat, digging through her bags, I could feel the tightness of the space, closing in on me. I forced myself to stop and think. If she were sitting down... She might have kept an EpiPen in her pocket, but if it poked her uncomfortably in the tight quarters...she might have stuck it into the seat pocket in front of her.

I reached my hand in and pulled it out. "Got it. Can you apply it?"

In response, Della held out her hand. As soon as I handed it over, she bit the lid off with her teeth and injected the woman in the thigh. I recapped the EpiPen while Della gently rubbed the injection site, something that would help the medicine disperse faster.

Della kept the woman on her side with her breathing passage cleared while I took the pulse. It was slowing as I counted, down to safer levels. However, the woman was clearly still out of sorts, her breathing evening out but her eyes glazed.

"Let's get her to the front," Della said. "There's a seat free in first class. We'll be able to recline her there."

I carried the woman to the front and then left her in Della's care, along with another stewardess who met us there. Another man stepped forward to help. The air marshal. Nothing designated him so, but I could tell he was packing from his stance and the grim set of his mouth. Seriously late to the party. I shook my head but let him pass. *Fall asleep on the job?* I figured both the stewardess and the marshal had received rudimentary first-aid training and could at least support the woman until we landed.

So I made myself scarce and returned to my seat.

"Everything okay?" James asked.

"She had an EpiPen. Seemed okay, but…"

But what the hell did I know? She'd definitely get checked out by a doctor on the ground. My time in the army had taught me that human life was both incredibly strong and infinitely fragile. I had seen a man move a Humvee to get his friend out from under it. They both lived. And I had seen a guy die in a bar fight during shore leave. A single punch to the head, landed wrong on the concrete floor—lights out. I had learned not to take anything for granted, even the relative safety of American soil.

The rest of the flight continued without incident. The departure took a little longer than usual as they first escorted the woman off the plane. She was long gone with paramedics by the time I walked through the gangway.

Della was still there, speaking with another stewardess off to the side. I hoisted my bag on my shoulder and kept walking.

"Talk to her," James muttered from beside me.

"Not a chance. I have Chelsea waiting for me, remember?" And based on my rapid pulse and dry eyes, the time away had messed me up more than I'd thought. I was in no condition to be around a woman, neither the one I'd just met nor the one I'd left behind.

James snorted. "I didn't say take her into the bathroom for a quickie. Just talk to her."

I shook my head, at both the man's way of speaking and his suggestion.

So, I'd felt a little attraction for someone. No big deal. As James had said in his own way, we were away a long time. It was normal to look. But if I went over to speak to her, it wouldn't be as a passenger on her plane. It would be as a man interested in a woman.

I just kept walking.

JAMES SWEPT RACHEL up in a bear hug and gave her a

searing kiss. I turned my head away out of respect, though I saw plenty of people stopping to stare. They looked pretty great, I had to admit. Great enough that I felt the absence of someone in my own arms acutely, like a knife in my side. Despite some of the crude things he said, I knew James was head over heels for this girl.

Rachel had a hug for me too. "You been staying out of trouble?"

"Pretty much." Aside from the two gunshot wounds that had been patched up in the field. James had sewed up one of them.

"This guy's a hero." James grinned. "He even saved someone's life on the plane ride over."

I rolled my eyes. "Don't listen to a word he says."

"Oh, don't worry. I don't." But Rachel was looking at her boyfriend with pure affection.

It didn't go unnoticed by James, who pulled her in for a longer kiss. "Let's get out of here," he murmured, low enough to be for her ears only. I shifted on my feet, feeling like an intruder. The terminal was bustling with people meeting loved ones. Emotion all around, battering me like little pricks, more painful than stitches in the jungle.

I felt Rachel look at me, heard her soft whisper. Not the contents, but I could guess where this was going.

"Hey, man, you need a ride?" James delivered the offer casually, but we all knew what was at stake. The last time we'd met in the airport, Rachel had been standing beside Chelsea.

Wasn't gonna happen. That wasn't disappointment sinking in my gut, was it? Guess I really had thought she'd show up. I'd sent her my itinerary, just in case. *What a shmuck.*

"I'm sure she's on her way," I said, lying through my teeth. "Don't wait up for me."

Rachel looked worried. "You sure?"

James mostly looked impatient—no doubt to take Rachel home and get busy. And why not? The guy deserved his R & R. No point in holding them up just because I was having woman troubles.

"Don't worry about me," I said.

"I'm a little worried," James said. "But not because of Chelsea."

I knew what he meant. He meant he didn't like Chelsea. He also meant I was a walking target if anyone found out about the memory stick in my bag. No way was I gonna check in luggage with that little piece of intel. But no one knew I had that list, and I would keep it that way.

"Well, don't be," I said. "Seriously, you guys are chilling in a cold-ass airport just to hang out with me? I must look better than I thought."

"Fuck you," James said with his usual friendly nature, but in his eyes I saw the warning. The data on that stick could make a lot of powerful men nervous. The kind of men who asked questions with their guns and made inquiries with C4 explosives.

It had been risky to even keep the damn thing. When I'd told my commander about it, he'd quietly told me to lose it. But the potential reward was too rich to pass up. This was national-security stuff. This was *domestic* security stuff, the kind of thing that kept children safe and off the streets. All of that compared to my life. I had figured out a long time ago how little it was worth.

So I had defied a direct order. And I would have to identify a high-ranking official, someone I could be sure wouldn't turn around and sell the information, someone with enough of a fire under them to actually pursue the list through the proper channels.

"I'll call you," I said in concession. I definitely wanted James's help on this. That was the reason I'd told him about it. Best friends. Blood brothers. I could count on him to have my back.

He nodded. "In that case..."

"Yeah, yeah, get out of here."

I didn't have to tell them twice. After another hug from Rachel, they disappeared into the crowd.

Damn. After searching baggage claim and the pickup circle outside, I had to admit Chelsea wasn't coming. The area was sticky and hot with the exhaust of all the idling cars. Everywhere I looked there were happy, tearful reunions. Bags going into cars. Kisses across the seat before the car pulled away.

No Chelsea.

I tried calling again. Voice mail. After the beep, I said, "Hey, Chels, it's me. I'm at the airport. I got your message, but I... I was hoping you could come pick me up. We could talk... or not. Call me?"

Shmuck.

I crossed the little intersection to where a sign indicated cabs would stop. Unfortunately there were no yellow cars lined up. Nothing at all. It seemed weird in such a busy airport, but maybe a bunch of planes had just arrived. Or maybe I was in the wrong place.

But traipsing all over the airport at this moment felt suddenly... impossible. Whatever survival mechanism that sustained me through the mission had subsided, leaving me tired and broken. My legs felt like jelly, way too wobbly to support my overlarge frame. I sat—or collapsed—on a bench and dumped my duffel bag beside me. Hopefully a cab would pull up.

My eyes fell shut. I'd definitely found sleep in the middle of worse situations. It wouldn't be appropriate here, of course, but I didn't care about that anymore. It was beyond me to care.

Sleep didn't come.

I heard the soft squeal of breaks in front of me. Instead of a yellow car, it was an older model black truck. The window rolled down, revealing the flight attendant from the plane. *Della.*

She raised her eyebrows. "Hop in, soldier."

Scrubbing a hand over my face, I looked left and right. Everything was just as I'd thought. People meeting loved ones. No sign of Chelsea.

"What?" I said, mostly stalling.

"I said get in. I'll take you home."

I shifted on the seat, wishing my brain wasn't filled

with cotton. Was she hitting on me? I mean, clearly she was trying to pick me up, but was she also trying to *pick me up?* She was gorgeous, and I hadn't even looked in a mirror in days. Mostly because I wouldn't like what I saw. There was no reason to think she was interested in me that way.

As if to confirm it, she added, "Look, I can take you wherever you need to go. I don't feel comfortable leaving you here when you look like roadkill."

Right. So she wasn't interested in me that way.

Even so, if she were a man and I were a woman, the situation would not be entirely safe. But in this case, I was a giant fresh out of combat, and Della was a tiny little thing. Even if she did drive a big truck, I doubted she would turn out to be a serial killer. Stranger things had happened, but considering the sadistic assholes I'd just tangled with, it was a risk I could take.

My phone screen was still blank. No returned called. No texts.

I let out a breath. "Do you know where the cabs line up? I saw the sign for here, but…"

"They moved that to Terminal C. It got too crowded around here so they split it up. You would've had to follow the signs from the gate."

And I hadn't done that. I'd gone with James to the car pickup area, expecting Chelsea to be here. Hoping she'd be here, the same way she'd been here the last time I'd come back from overseas. That was probably stupid, but this last undercover thing had been rougher than I'd expected, rougher than I *could* have expected.

The final weeks of army training were supposed to be tough. The training for spec ops was supposed to be tougher. But nothing had prepared me for the sight of kids being used. Nothing prepared me for not being able to do a damn thing to help them. Instead I had to gather evidence, to shoot the shit with the scum of the earth and *laugh* about it. So yeah, I'd played the fool here, and the pretty stewardess got to witness it.

"I'll chip in for gas," I said.

She smiled. "You don't have to do that."

I pulled open the door, tossed my duffel bag to the backseat and climbed in. "I have a girlfriend."

It wasn't the smoothest delivery. Nor was it strictly true, considering I'd been dumped. But I needed to talk to Chelsea before I really knew what was going on. I needed closure. And I wouldn't take the chance of leading Della on that something could happen. She deserved better than some strung-out army grunt on the rebound.

Grimacing, I chanced a look.

She raised a perfectly arched eyebrow. "In that case, I'll let you chip in for gas."

# Chapter Three
## Della

H E WAS SILENT for the first five miles we drove. Once he told me what part of town he lived in, he'd shut down. It might have been insulting, the way he barely spoke to me, how he refused to make a move. Even if he did have a girlfriend waiting for him.

What was I going to do about her?

His eyes were closed. Was he sleeping? But no, I could feel his presence vibrating through the air in my truck. It had been like that in the airplane too, his vitality like waves that could lap at my cheeks. His large body swayed gently with the motion of the truck. That relaxed pose was a facade, something that would fool a lesser fighter into thinking he was unaware.

But I had plenty of experience with men's bodies. I knew how they looked when stalking their prey. I knew how they looked at the height of climax. This man had been through hell and back, and I knew that look too.

Cuts marred his tanned cheek and neck. Something had made a gauge at the back of his neck, leaving a scab still puffy with irritation. Heavy shadows marred his eyes, almost as heavy as a bruise, dark slashes beneath his golden lashes.

*Kind eyes.* I had learned to recognize those too.

A bright sign for a drive-up fast food place passed us by, and I exited the freeway.

"Where are we going?" he asked, his voice husky with exhaustion.

"Figured you could use some lunch. You look hungry." More than hungry. He looked like he needed... everything. Food. Sleep. Even air itself. If I'd met him a different way, I would have wanted to give him those things, to care for him. To protect him.

Which was funny, considering.

He shook his head. "I'm okay."

"Come on. It won't bite." I maneuvered the truck beneath the small overhang carport and rolled down the window. "When's the last time you ate, anyway? I know they didn't serve lunch on the plane."

"I had coffee..." He scrubbed his face with a hand. "A few hours ago."

"Proving my point, soldier. A big boy like you needs nourishment."

He gave me a strange look, as if he couldn't figure out if I was flirting with him. Maybe when he figured that out, he could tell me, because even I wasn't sure. What I did know was that I couldn't fight him. Despite the obvious toll his trip had taken, he was alert. His fists were huge, his muscles clearly defined beneath the army-green shirt he wore. No, the only weapon I had against him was sexuality.

What else was new?

"I'll take a burger," he conceded. "And whatever's the biggest soda they have."

Yeah, he'd probably take an IV injection of caffeine if they had one. He was battling sleep big-time. But he needed rest. Caffeine wouldn't be good for him. It wouldn't be good for my purposes either.

I leaned out the window and ordered three burgers and an extra-large lemonade. He raised his eyebrows at the change in his order, but he didn't complain. Naturally submissive. I could tell these things, often after speaking with someone for a minute. That wasn't conceit talking. In my old job I only had a minute to figure a guy out. That skill helped in my new job too.

Girlfriend or not, he wasn't immune to me. He thought I was looking at the menu, but out of the corner of my eye, I saw his gaze, hungry and a little desperate, on my body. The blue airline uniform was stiff and unappealing, but he made me feel like I was dressed in silk. Not even the cheap, gaudy kind, but something luxurious.

His voice was gruff when he spoke. "So... how'd a nice girl like you end up in this dirty business?"

Surprise forced all the air from my lungs. "What?" I managed to get out.

He nodded toward the badge still stuck to my chest, the one with gold airplane wings and the name *Della*. "Charging fifty bucks to check in a bag. Holding us hostage during layovers. It's practically highway robbery."

"Oh." The air suddenly liquefied again, rushing into my lungs like a waterfall.

His brows drew together. Was that concern? God, it had been so long since anyone had worried about me. No, it had never happened.

"Sorry," he muttered. "Bad joke."

"Don't apologize." I tried to smile. "You're right. They're pretty evil about it. But I have to admit, they've taken good care of me." The pay sucked, but the health benefits were stellar. No risk of getting raped or killed, for example. That definitely improved my well-being.

"That's good." The sleepiness had drained from his eyes, leaving only a piercing intensity that seemed to see right through me.

I shifted in my seat and looked away. *Point one for soldier boy.*

"Did you always want to fly?" he asked softly.

A knot formed in my throat, and I swallowed around it. *Point two.* I may not come out the winner in this match. But then, that was the point, wasn't it? Dmitri thought I was going to die on the mission he'd given me. Maybe so, but I'd go down fighting.

"Yeah," I said, just as quietly. "I always wanted to get away. No one can touch you in the sky, right?"

He caught the steel in my voice. His eyes sharpened into blades; they cut me open. I bled onto the steering wheel, all over the console beside me. All the while thinking *touch me, touch me, touch me.* A lifetime of bartering with my body had left me broken inside, unable to tell the difference between lust and affection. Or maybe I could always tell the difference. That was why it hurt so damn much.

A knock on the window startled me. I let out a small shriek, then blushed, embarrassed. Warmth covered my hand, and I looked down to see his larger hand over mine. Comforting me.

Drawing in a breath, I pulled away. There would be time enough for that. He'd touch me plenty more places before we were through. Every one outside my body, but nowhere inside me. I wouldn't let him touch me there. I paid for the food and rolled my window up. The business of brown paper wrapping and straws were the distraction I needed to pull myself together.

✧   ✧   ✧

WE GOT BACK on the road quickly. I watched with some fascination as he scarfed down the burgers, the sight of his throat swallowing strangely compelling. Or maybe not so strangely. I knew my tastes in men ran to the perverse. But I was used to dealing with smaller men, ones with slender hands and hips. The kind I could lock between my legs until he convinced me to let him go.

Clint would be nothing like that. He had enough power in his pinky finger to level me. And the thought of all that power being wiped away... My stomach turned over.

But it wasn't a guarantee he would die. He could defend himself—better than I ever could. And I was well-accustomed to do-or-die situations.

As in, I did what Dmitri said or my sister died.

"You want one?" Clint held up a foil-wrapped burger.

Shaking my head, I put the truck in gear. "No, thanks."

"Are you sure? A big girl like you needs nourishment." His low voice was teasing, and despite myself, I smiled. We both knew he outweighed me by a hundred pounds, but the low tenor of his voice when he called me a *big girl* told me he wasn't talking about my size. He was talking about sex. But playfully. Without the hint of coercion I was used to. *Damn.*

And did he have to be so cute? I didn't want to find him adorable. I didn't want to like him at all. This would be so much easier if he were a sleazeball like Dmitri.

My phone buzzed in my purse, and I pulled it out. *Well?*

One word and my heart plummeted. Dmitri. He wanted to know if I'd gotten the man named Clint Adams, the one who'd been sitting in seat 34B. Uh, yeah, I had him, but Dmitri had neglected to mention that man would be in combat gear. Clearly he was in one of the military branches, which made him extra dangerous. It also meant he served his country, and I had a lot of respect for that.

Enough respect to let my sister die?

I texted back one-handed at a red light. *Working on it.*

Because I didn't have this all worked out. In a few minutes we'd arrive at his house, where his girlfriend would no doubt be. Not a very good girlfriend, I thought with some disgust, since she hadn't bothered to come pick him up. But I could hardly be jealous, considering. At least she wasn't going to get him killed.

"You okay?" he murmured.

"Yeah, sure."

"Because you seem a little... agitated."

I glanced down and realize I'd been gripping the steering wheel so hard my knuckles were white. Yeah, I was agitated. I'd done a lot of crazy shit for Dmitri, but this one definitely took the mafia cake. What would happen if I just started driving toward Dmitri's safe house right now? Obviously the guy would notice a detour into the seedy part of town. I needed Clint immobilized, unconscious, and that was impossible with him alert and powerful and studying me from across the truck.

He seemed to lean away from me, almost trying to make himself small. Which was ridiculous. That would never work, as big as he was. He filled the whole cab, right up to my face, where I breathed in his musky scent. My skin tingled whenever he looked at me—all the time. Whenever I was in sight of him, I felt his gaze on me, hot and surprisingly sweet.

"I thought maybe you'd changed your mind about driving me." He shrugged. "You don't know me, but I'd never hurt you."

I blinked, incredulous. He thought I was *scared* of him. God. *God.* I couldn't do this. My throat closed up. "I know," I managed to say. And the strangest part was that I *did* know he wouldn't hurt me. How many men could I say that about? Only him.

"But if you wanted to pull over somewhere, I could call a cab. No problem. I don't mind."

I just shook my head. Stupidly, tears were forming. Why couldn't he stop being nice to me? I wanted him to hit me, to fight me. I wanted him to tear me down or submit to me. This good-guy angle was too much for me, like a dream I didn't know I'd had.

*Your sister needs you.*

With pure will I forced myself to calm. Why was he affecting me like this? That was a problem I hadn't expected when I'd reluctantly agreed to do this. But I sucked in a deep breath and blew it out shakily.

I glanced at the screen of my phone. It had gone dark. "I was just looking up a map. But you can tell me where to go."

He directed me off the freeway and through a network of streets without any other kind words, to my relief. We finally pulled up to an aging apartment complex. Despite the obvious wear on the buildings, tall trees provided shade over the cobblestone walkway. A cat sat licking his paw on one of the flower beds. It was a quaint place, both rustic and comfortable—kind of like the man himself.

He handed me a couple of bills. I split them with a slide of my fingers. Two twenties. "This is too much," I protested.

"Nah. It should be more, considering the gas and the

food. And your time. That's all I have on me."

"Clint, I can't take all your money."

Something flickered in his eyes. Was that pain? "How did you know my name?"

*Shit.* I'd given myself away. But instead of feeling broken up about it, I was glad. Glad he'd caught me. Glad he'd stay safe. "The flight roster," I whispered.

"You always memorize it?" he asked jokingly.

"Because of the incident," I forced out. "I had to make an incident report for the woman on the plane. So I looked up your name."

He seemed to accept that explanation. He reached for his neck and pulled out a set of silver tags. "Army Sergeant Clint Adams, at your service."

My gaze lingered on those two flat pieces of metal. As if I'd voiced the request, he pulled the chain over his head and handed it over. It was heavier than I'd expected, and warm from his body. I ran my thumb over the lettering. *Adams, Clint F.*

"F?" I asked.

"Fitzgerald." His cheeks turned a faint pink. "An old family name."

He volunteered so much. Not just his name, rank and serial number. He gave me his history, his kindness. He gave and gave and gave until I felt sick with how much more I would take from him. I ran the chain over my hand, tangling my fingers through the beaded metal as if it was his hair. Then drawing up tight, capturing us both.

He started to speak, then stopped. Then started again,

seeming hesitant. "You were amazing, you know. Smooth under pressure. Not everyone could have reacted that quickly."

I had a lot of experience administering needles to convulsing people. Though mostly that was my sister going through violent withdrawals. What did that make me? Not *amazing,* that was for sure. An enabler, probably. But I couldn't stand to see her suffer. I did anything to get that needle from Dmitri, and then I used it to give her a few hours of peace.

That was my old life. My new life, as a flight attendant, was supposed to be about making an honest wage. But nothing was ever that simple.

"I appreciated your help," I said.

"Listen, what I said before about having a..." He glanced behind him, toward the faded door to his apartment building. His expression was torn as he cleared his throat. "I really appreciate the ride."

What had he been about to say? It was probably better that I didn't know. *I don't actually have a girlfriend. And oh, by the way, do you want to come have sex?* I didn't want to see him lie to me just so he could bang me later when his girlfriend wasn't looking. I didn't want him to invite me up to an empty apartment while I ignored the signs that he didn't live alone. That was the sort of dick move I'd expect from any other guy—but not him. Even if it would help me hurt him, I didn't want to hate him.

"Take care, Della," he said finally.

"Take care," I repeated softly.

He hefted his bag and shut the door. My muscles tensed, straining to go after him. Not because of the way he affected me, but because I needed him. My sister's safety depended on him. For years I had done everything in the name of her safety. But I watched him walk away, with no plans for how to get back in his life.

# CHAPTER FOUR

## CLINT

I T PHYSICALLY HURT to walk away from her. Crazy but true. I wanted her to drive me away from here and the confrontation no doubt waiting for me inside my apartment. But at least Della could be comfortable now. She had been downright squirming by the last five minutes. She probably had a million things to do, and none of them were to babysit my tired ass.

I stalked up the sidewalk and stepped inside. The door to the building led to a dim hallway. I kept my head down, gaze trained on the thinly carpeted stairs... and almost tripped over the box blocking the hallway at the top. Sure enough, the entire landing was full of stuff.

My stuff. *Fuck.*

There were about seven large cardboard boxes. My bicycle. She'd put my TV out? Jesus. Annoyed now, I slung my duffel bag on top of everything and picked my way across the wreckage. That was just my luck. James got to go home and snuggle up with his girl. I was climbing over all my worldly possessions as if it were rocky terrain on enemy territory.

I raised my hand to knock, and the door opened.

She looked… seriously pissed.

"Hey, Chels."

"Don't 'Hey, Chels' me. It took you long enough to get home."

Seriously? "Well, I hadn't arranged a ride. I thought you'd be picking me up."

"Did you not get my text?"

*Jesus.*

Suddenly I felt like the dumbest of dumb-asses. I should've taken the Dear John texts more seriously, but I hadn't wanted to. It was easier to pretend everything was okay, even when she wouldn't answer my calls, even when she hadn't shown up at the airport. Easier to pretend she hadn't just poured salt on the very real wounds currently aching all over my body.

But those black-on-white words had felt unreal somehow, as if the world had gone sideways while I was tucked away in the darkest corner of the world. I kept waiting to wake up and find everything how I left it. My gut tightened. But clearly she was serious about breaking up. Her expression was more derisive than anything else.

"Yeah, I got your text," I said tiredly. "But if you're so keen on breaking up, why are you still in my apartment? More to the point, why is all my stuff in the hallway?"

"Oh, *your* apartment. Is that how you're gonna play this?"

And I definitely wasn't going to say, *I thought we could work it out.* Because regardless of what delusions I'd been harboring on the flight over, I didn't want to work it out anymore. Maybe it was meeting Della. Maybe it was the shock of seeing all my shit piled up like trash. Whatever the reason, I was finally on the same page.

It was over.

"Well… yeah. I mean, I've been paying the rent, so…"

She laughed. "Great. So this is about money now."

"What? No. I mean, I told you I didn't mind you staying here, and I never asked you to chip in."

"But you're asking now, right? You're going to hold it over me?"

Frustration rose up like acid. "*No.* Shit. I'm not trying to hold anything over you. I'm just trying to catch up here. And maybe get a few hours of sleep somewhere in this forty-eight-hour period."

"You can take your stuff and go somewhere else. I'm the one who's been living here for the past six months. Not you."

"But…" I shook my head. My stomach churned with nausea, threatening to eject the three burgers I'd had on the way over. "My name's on the lease."

She flinched. "Are you going to kick me out?"

How did I end up the bad guy here? I felt like some sort of asshole stalker, bothering this girl when she clearly didn't want me here. Except… this was actually my apartment. But maybe she had a point. She'd gotten settled here, and I hadn't. Obviously. I looked around at my stuff, coming up around my legs like quicksand. Always the drifter. Always the reject. This place was supposed to be some kind of stability for me. I'd gotten the lease and paid it in full, knowing I'd be gone. And when Chelsea had roommate troubles and asked to move in, it had seemed like another step in the right direction. Putting down roots. Making a home.

But… hell. A heavy weight inside my chest felt all too familiar. Her expression said it all. *You're not wanted here.*

"I'm not gonna make you leave," I said gruffly. "I'm not gonna do anything to you. Can I just leave my stuff here for a couple of days? I don't have another place lined up."

She shook her head firmly. "No way."

Suddenly understanding clicked into place, like a vice around my lungs. "You got some guy here, don't you?"

"Of course not," she said. But the furious blush on her face said otherwise.

"He may not be here right now, but he comes around, right? Just tell me this. Was it before or after you sent that text?"

Her mouth set in stubborn lines I was familiar with. *Before.* That was the answer she didn't say. Fuck, it shouldn't hurt. It shouldn't feel like a knife in my back that she'd been cheating on me. I swayed on my feet and leaned against the doorjamb. A fucking fight when I thought I was safe. I never could get used to that.

A softy. A sucker. A punching bag for anyone with a bone to pick until I got big enough to defend myself.

She stepped forward, her expression softening. Her hand extended. "Clint…"

"Don't worry about it," I said. *Back the fuck off,* I didn't say.

Yeah, so I wasn't exactly over it. I'd get there, but at this second I felt like the world's biggest chump. *Sure, you can live with me. No, you don't have to pay any rent. And okay, go right head and fucking cheat on me while I'm getting shot at, why don't you.*

"Clint, do you—"

"Just go." I gestured roughly for the door she still held. "I'll figure something out. Not your problem."

She had the gall to look wounded. But at least she did what I said, so I could slump against the rail and look weak without her seeing. We'd never had the kind of crazy love that James and Rachel had, but I always thought that wasn't for me. I was perfectly fine with something safe and predictable…until it wasn't anymore.

Focus, soldier.

And now I had to figure out where to put a bunch of stuff. In storage? How fast could I get another apartment? I'd be extending myself with rent on two places, but hell, I didn't really have a choice. Kicking Chelsea out was something I wouldn't do no matter how mad I was. And I wasn't exactly relishing the thought of sleeping where she'd fucked some other guy anyway. She could keep the bed.

I climbed back over the boxes and stopped short at the top of the stairs. Standing at the bottom was Della.

"Hi," she said meekly. She had her arms wrapped around her chest, hugging herself.

From her expression she would have preferred to be anywhere but here. And God, I wanted that too. Humili- ation poured through me, molten lava that left only charred earth in its wake. She had heard all of that, everything. She knew exactly what Chelsea had done while I'd been overseas.

Being cheated on and dumped had been pretty terri- ble. Knowing the pretty flight attendant had witnessed the whole thing made me want to punch something. Like my fucking TV beside me, for starters.

"What are you doing here?" My voice came out raw, as if I'd been partying last night and then spent the morning hunched around the ceramic bowl. Instead of what I'd really done, which was spend over twenty-four hours on a series of connecting flights to get back to a place that wasn't my home anymore.

She held up a set of dog tags. "Thought you might need these."

"Right." And I'd left my identification with a virtual stranger. Excellent. I couldn't catch a break.

Pushing myself forward, I made it down the stairs. When I grasped the tags dangling from her hand, she tightened her grip. I raised my eyebrow in question, connected to her through the light metal.

"What're you gonna do?" she murmured.

Damn her sweet Southern accent. "Haven't figured that out yet."

She peered around me. "Got a lot of stuff?"

"Enough." Maybe if I was short with her, she'd leave

me the hell alone.

"I was thinking…" Her lashes lowered before her lush brown gaze met mine again. "I was thinking you could stay with me."

Or maybe not.

I grabbed the back of my neck and squeezed, hoping it would dislodge the hundred-pound weight pressed there. Didn't help. "Stay with you," I repeated hollowly.

She shrugged. "You'll have somewhere to put your stuff while you find another place."

I made a noncommittal sound. "And what'll you get?"

Her gaze dipped down, sliding along my chest and lower, lower, to where I'd suddenly begun to harden. Fuck, that was hot. Incredibly, impossibly hot to see her look at me like I was a slab of meat and she was a god-damned lioness. And I wanted to get eaten—oh, I surely did. Had wanted that since I'd first caught a glimpse of her walking toward me down the airplane aisle.

But I was a fucking mess, my heart ripped out and hung up to drain. And physically too. I hadn't had a decent night's sleep in months. Though the bruises on my torso were mostly healed, the graze of a bullet kept me hopped up on painkillers even now.

If she was looking for a good time… she should look somewhere else.

"Della… I appreciate the offer. Seriously appreciate it. To be blunt with you, my situation is fucked up right now, and I don't want to pull you into this."

She stepped forward, bringing our faces mere inches

apart. If I leaned a little ways, we would be kissing.

"Hey," she murmured, "the offer wasn't made lightly. I know all about fucked-up situations, and if I could make yours a little easier, I'd consider it worth it."

I should say no. I knew that. I should lug all this stuff to some monthly rental storage place and then bunker down in a cheap motel that smelled like smoke and worse things. But here was a beautiful girl offering to solve all my problems, and damned if I could resist.

✧   ✧   ✧

DELLA LIVED IN a small white house with a wood porch swing. Honeysuckle climbed up the pillars and filled the air with a sweet scent. Her neighborhood featured lush green grass and not a fence in sight. A palm tree sagged in the front yard, clearly in need of trimming. But otherwise the house looked no worse for her absence. The porch light lit the steps in the waning evening.

"Nice place," I said.

She glanced back at me, her smile almost sad. "Thanks."

I rocked on my heels, disconcerted by the sense of unwelcome. As if she wanted me to leave. I got that from her sometimes. One minute she'd be checking me out and inviting me over. The next she'd withdraw, leaving only the shell of the pretty girl behind. I couldn't figure her out. But then again, my brain had stopped functioning sometime this morning. Right now I was running on fumes. Oh, and lust. My attraction for her had only grown with the realization that I might actually get to act on it. I just hoped I didn't pass out in the middle. Boy, I sure knew how to impress a girl.

She flicked on the light, revealing a comfortable dining room connected to the living room. Pointing to an open space between them, she said, "Not much privacy, but you can put your stuff there. There should be enough room."

"If you're sure…"

The corners of her mouth lifted into a grin, a real one. "Backing out already, soldier? Where's your follow-through?"

Damn, I liked it when she teased me. When she emerged from that shell and bared herself in that way, hints of humor and light.

"I'll go get my stuff from the truck. But just to be clear, I'm paying to stay here." When she pursed her lips, clearly prepared to argue, I shook my head. "Let's plan on a week, and we'll figure out the fair rate for that."

Her eyes grew clouded, darkened by some secret she hadn't yet revealed. "A week ought to be just long enough, soldier."

If only I knew why it sounded ominous, more like a threat than a promise.

I put the boxes and my bicycle in her garage, ignoring the unease in my gut. I flashed back to when she'd pulled up in front of me, offering me a ride. If the situation were reversed, if I were a woman and she were a man, maybe I'd better be careful. But considering the circumstances, that kind of wariness felt silly. Even exhausted and mildly injured, I was a trained soldier. While she was... a beautiful woman. One who could find a date in any bar in town. The fact that she'd dragged my sorry ass home was pure charity.

The hot water in the shower found every bruise and open cut, burning before soothing away the sting. The walls seemed to sway in front of my eyes. I had a faint hope I wouldn't slip and crack my head open. It would hardly be good behavior for a guest. But I stepped out of her small, steam-filled bathroom without incident. At least the steady spray had done its best to pound out the knots in my shoulders. I wanted to dive directly into bed, but instead I slung on sweatpants and a T-shirt, the fabric clinging to my still-wet skin.

The duffel bag wasn't outside the door where I'd left it.

Someone was humming. The sound was low and melodic, whispering beneath my skin and raising goose bumps in its wake. It sounded almost familiar. Not a song I'd heard before, but it filled a space inside me, as if I had been waiting to hear it.

I followed the haunting sound to the bedroom, where my duffel bag had taken up residence in an antique-looking chair against the wall. Della was pulling down the comforter from the bed, such a sweetly domestic movement that my chest grew tight.

She stopped humming.

Her smile appeared shy. "You can sleep in here."

I took another step into the room. White walls, white sheets. Dark brown knotted wood flooring. "Is this your room?"

"Of course not. I'm across the hall."

That sense of reversal washed over me again, the way a man might make a woman feel safe, the way he'd reassure her he wouldn't take advantage. She was doing the same for me—making me feel safe. Assuring me she wouldn't require me to have sex with her, which was really ironic considering I'd give anything to touch her. Or be touched.

The way she was so competent everywhere, so thoughtful and caring…it made me think she'd mess me up. Not physically. Emotionally. She'd touch me just right. It wouldn't matter where on my body or with what part of hers. It would be the quiet assurance, the focused affection that would undo me.

I'd had my share of sex before, but I'd never had anyone turn down the sheets for me to sleep.

"Who usually sleeps here?" I asked.

She glanced around at the bare walls and frilly curtains. "No one, I guess. It's a guest room. Although…sometimes my sister stays here." Her lashes veiled her eyes. "You can stand in for her."

My feelings toward Della were decidedly unsisterly. "Where is she now?"

Those brown eyes met mine, and the pain in them stole my breath away. "I don't know."

"Shit. I'm sorry."

Her lips pressed together. Shadows moved over her slender throat as she swallowed. I got the impression she was trying to get herself under control, and I regretted my line of questioning. Wasn't it enough that she'd opened her home to me? She'd given me her trust, and I'd gone and dredged up painful thoughts.

She shook her head. "It's not your fault. That's the thing about family. They're connected to you, even when they're not."

"That sounds...really good."

Her gaze sharpened. "Do you have brothers or sisters?"

"No. No family." I hesitated. "I grew up in a group home."

Sympathy flashed through her eyes. "That must have been hard."

"Not too bad." I hadn't minded the repetitive meals or the small beds. I *had* minded the older boys who tried to take advantage, but I learned how to fight dirty even as a child. Then I got big, and no one had managed to best me since.

She stepped closer and placed her hand on my arm. Just there, the lightest touch of fingertips to my forearm. I felt the impact like a blow, electric rain on my skin, a form of torture I never wanted to end.

"I'm sorry." Her voice had dropped low. There was an undercurrent there, something I couldn't figure out yet. As if she wasn't apologizing for my past...

Then what? I wanted to decode her. As if she were an

encrypted message we'd picked up from insurgents. But unlike the enemies I worked against, I would never use that knowledge against her.

My throat felt dry. "What if I don't want to sleep alone?"

She smiled, the hint of mocking almost soothing. "Soldier, you look like you're about to fall asleep standing up. You don't have the energy to do anything *but* sleep."

Yeah, sex was probably out of the question. I had a semi being in the same room with her, but just because I had the equipment didn't mean I should use it. Two days of no sleep had left me strung tight. And despite my exhaustion, I didn't expect that to change anytime soon. Every time I closed my eyes, I was back in that fucking warehouse.

She began caressing me, so light I almost didn't notice it. Except for the way I hardened to full mast. And damn, that was clearly visible beneath the fleece fabric of my pants. But she wasn't looking between my legs. Her eyes were trained on mine.

"It's more than just being tired, isn't it?" she whispered.

I swallowed thickly. "Yeah."

"Do you want to talk about it?"

"I can't." It was classified, for one thing. But even if I could've shared it, I never would've told her about the things I'd seen. There was no reason to give her nightmares too.

Though judging from the shadows in her eyes, she

had her own nightmares.

"Lie down in the bed, soldier."

"Della?"

"That's an order."

Fuck, why was that so hot? I couldn't help the streaks of lust that ran through me. Couldn't do anything but obey her. Was it the tiredness making my skin overly sensitive? The slide of fleece against my skin, the embroidered eyelet duvet beneath my palms. The world felt more textured, more vibrant when she was in it.

The bed creaked as I climbed on, and I looked back, waiting to see if she'd follow.

She did, thank God. I breathed pure relief while she placed a knee on the bed, her eyes dark and implacable. Her face was all shadows, but I could see her clearly in my mind. The polite smile she'd given me on the plane. The more playful one through the window of her truck. And then she was in front of me, where I still couldn't see her smile—but I could feel it, curved and wicked when it met my lips in a kiss.

# Chapter Five
## Della

WHAT WAS I doing with him? I should leave him alone. I should call Dmitri right now and tell him where to go. Hell, I could even tie Clint up before Dmitri got here, a pretty little package. Though Clint wasn't little. Not at all. It was like climbing a mountain just to straddle him. And when I got there? The air was thin at the peak. I couldn't breathe, couldn't think, couldn't feel anything except an irrational sense of triumph.

The man could kiss. For just a moment, when my lips touched his, he froze. A sound vibrated from deep in his chest, rumbling surprise over the hills and valleys of his pecs. I didn't know why he should be surprised. With a body like that, he would attract the attention of any girl with a pulse. The way he seemed to put everyone else's comfort above his own would seal the deal.

I nipped at his bottom lip and reveled in his answering groan.

"Honey," he muttered, and that alone, the endearment, was enough to make me clench.

Just a shimmy of my hips would be enough to center me over him. I'd push the thick cloth of his sweatpants aside and then I'd be riding him, taking us both to oblivion. But something held me back. A conscience? He was exhausted. I could see the redness of his eyes and the shadows underneath. His body reacted with a sluggish lust, eager but far too gone.

That was okay, though. I could do all the work.

I was used to that.

His chest was broad. Open plains for my lips to roam. *Amber waves of grain,* I thought with a private smile. He was the all-American boy, my soldier. Sometimes you had to make a choice. Dmitri loomed in the back of my mind with his orders and his threats. Right now I chose this. I licked his nipple until it was a tight, puckered nub. The sound he made was pure masculine pleasure, and that's what I chose.

"Do you like that?" I purred.

"No... *Yes...* You don't have to..."

His pecs bulged, muscles sharply cut, and I used that angle to bite him. He jerked beneath me but did nothing to protect himself. So damned trusting. Way too sweet for the likes of me. "Who said that was for you? Maybe I just want to play."

He groaned. "Oh God. *Della.*"

My name on his lips made me wet. Oh, who was I kidding? I was already soaking my panties. Just looking at him had done that. Scenting his musk and feeling his presence. The man had the body of a god but the fragile mortality of a man. His heart thumped steadily beneath my palm. I pushed myself up, straddling his hips.

I should get him off quickly and be done with it. No, I should leave him alone right now. But instead I wanted to stay and take my time. It was the kind of sexual play I dreamed of, alone, at night with my vibrator in hand. Wonder of wonders, he seemed to be getting off on it. The man was clearly alpha on a battlefield. He got wary looks from the other men at the airport—even they understood the sensual power he radiated. But here, between my thighs, he liked it when I teased him.

"Are you too tired, soldier? Should I let you rest now?"

His hips jerked. Oh yes, he liked being teased. "If you want," he panted.

I took mercy on him and lifted my shirt over my head, baring my breasts. It was an embossed invitation, written with calligraphy and overlaid with vellum. *Do what you want with me. I'm yours for the night.* He looked. It practically left a trail of fire over my pale, exposed skin, that's how hotly he looked at my breasts. But he didn't touch. His hands lay at his sides, twitching once and then lying still.

Letting me call the shots.

My finger trailed down his chest, winding a lonely path down the furred skin. Golden-dark hair made a trail for me to follow, an arrow pointing where I needed to go. Even his hip bones formed a V, showing me the way. I scooted my knees back so that I straddled his legs.

His thighs were wider than his waist had been, bulging with muscles that had helped him defend and invade, protect and conquer. He was a warrior in every way—even the way he trembled with restraint. It would have been so easy to flip me over and shove himself inside me. Other men would have done so. Lesser men.

His lips parted. His lids were low with hunger. "Della?"

"I'm here."

*Here* was my fingers tugging down the elastic waistband, letting his cock spring free. *Here* was circling his cock with my thumb and forefinger, a slight grip that propped him up more than stroked him. *Here* was a lick from the base of his cock to the tip.

"Oh fuck."

My lips curved into a smile, but I didn't let that stop me as I covered the head of his cock with my mouth. The underside met in a ridge that I teased with my tongue. He was already salty, already damp with his own seed, so I licked it off until he tasted like nothing at all.

"Baby, that feels so good. Oh Jesus. Let me... let me..."

He didn't finish asking for permission, so I didn't give it. Whatever he wanted, it wouldn't be better than this. His hips were already jerking up, shoving his cock roughly into my mouth, a helpless response to pleasure.

I paused long enough to tell him, "Don't come yet."

Then I took him deep, sliding my lips down his wide cock as far as I could. I pulled back and tried to go deeper the next time. I was still plenty far from the dark hairs at the base of his groin. He was just too big to take all of him. Not only long, but also thick, as if all that physical training had also exercised his cock. I imagined dirty drill sergeants and mandatory repetitions and somehow felt even more turned on.

This man pushed every one of my buttons. Even exhausted and temporarily homeless, he was the most alluring man I'd ever met. If he ever actually *tried* to seduce me, I'd probably melt into a puddle. That was me, the Wicked Witch of the West, destroyed out of a misguided sense of loyalty to my sister.

My sucking fell into a rhythm we could both recognize: the rocking of sex and the sea, the moonlit tides guiding my head as I bobbed up and down. He grunted on every downward slide, the same way he would if he was plunging into my pussy.

"Come here." His voice was hoarse like gravel. "Turn around. Let me lick you."

Oh, good boy. He'd managed to bring himself to ask. And I wanted to reward that kind of initiative, I really did. I was sure he'd be talented in that arena. My sex clenched at the thought of his eager tongue lapping away.

But despite the haze of lust around us, I remembered why he was here. Tomorrow I would betray him. He'd never again look at me with both desire and tenderness. He'd never look at me at all.

If nothing else, I could give him this.

I leaned back, resting on his legs. My lips felt swollen from sucking him. My nipples were tight with arousal. "You don't give the orders around here. Now, you're going to lie there and take your lumps like a good solider. Got it?"

Something dark flashed in his eyes. I thought he might refuse.

"Yes, ma'am," he said curtly.

My whole body went rigid, aching to ram something. Ideally, him. I wasn't alone in that reaction. God, he was so turned on. I watched his cock twitch with intense fascination. My cunt clenching and his cock flexing. When they finally slid together, it would be a violent intercourse, and that made me want it even more.

*Would he fuck you if he knew why you'd lured him here?*

No, and he wouldn't let me suck him off either, but I wasn't about to tell him anything.

I put my finger to my mouth and got it nice and wet. His eyes widened. He knew what was coming next. His body tensed, a reflexive move to keep me out. I could have punished him for that, but I decided to reward him instead, with my mouth on his cock again. He *should* learn to protect himself. Even if it was too little, too late.

I licked and sucked his hot cock, making sure no inch of skin went unloved. He would be damp with my saliva, coated completely. I hoped the air was cool against wet skin when I pulled back, a sharp contrast to the heat of my mouth when I engulfed him. However it felt, he seemed to enjoy it. He groaned so loud it filled the air, a kind of roaring despair that reminded me of my order to him.

Don't come yet.

And this man could obey orders. It became a challenge between us, to see if I could get him to come without giving permission. I recognized that it wouldn't be quite fair that way, but I didn't care. I licked and sucked and nibbled at him. I slid my fist up and down his length. I sneaked a finger down against his puckered hole and pressed inside.

He shot up from the bed, shouting incoherently. Then, "God. *God*. That feels... I don't know. Ahhh, baby."

It was only when I went deeper that he gripped the sheets, almost tearing them in his fervor. "Come now," I whispered, so quietly he might not have heard me. But then he was coming, with a tortured cry and hot spurts of seed onto my tongue.

I swallowed him down, drinking the come and nuzzling his softening cock until he slumped back to the bed. He was breathing hard, but his eyes were closed. His limbs were sprawled as if I'd knocked him unconscious. And maybe I had.

He made a soft sound, almost a worrisome sound. I brushed my hand over his forehead. "Shh. Rest."

Then I gently pulled his sweatpants up over his cock. I settled the blanket around his waist. And I tucked him into bed with a kiss to his forehead. The whole time, he barely moved to help me. His breathing evened out. His eyes opened once, focused on me, and then the lids slammed shut once again.

By the time I left his room, he was already asleep.

✧ ✧ ✧

I WOULDN'T BE able to sleep anytime soon. My body was a jumble of nerves—arousal and guilt and fear forming a Molotov cocktail inside me. I headed to the kitchen for a small cup of tea. My hands trembled as I prepared it, the cup rattling against the dish until I set it on the table.

The house was fifty years old. Caro didn't understand why I'd picked this one when I could have had a newer one for the same price. She didn't see the value in original hardwood floors and a wide, plush lawn. The house had character, and that made it a home. A place where I could get comfortable and put down roots. I'd been waiting my whole life to put down roots.

But then, Caro was comparing it to whatever mansion Dmitri had kept her in. No doubt it had glass tables and expensive artwork and guards with machine guns. He liked to think he was highbrow.

I had actually been glad when he upgraded from head gangbanger to major crime boss. He'd hooked up with some other guys and started dealing bigger. *International business opportunities,* he'd said with a smirk. He had started to travel more and released his hold on me and Caro.

The only problem was, Caro wouldn't let go of him. She wanted that lifestyle. As sleazy as he was, she wanted *him.* Sometimes that pissed me off. Those days I'd think about cutting her loose. But most of the time I remembered that neither of us had chosen to go with him. We had been thrown into hell together, and I was the only one who had escaped. She was my sister. I wouldn't let her down.

My phone rang, startling me. Tea sloshed over the rim of the cup as I set it down with a thud. My gaze snapped to the dark staircase. Would he hear?

I grabbed the phone from the table and slipped out the back door. The ambient sounds were louder here— singing crickets and rustling leaves and the soothing hum of nighttime.

"Hello?" I whispered.

"Della, it's me."

Relief made me feel faint. "Caro! Oh God, I've been so worried about you. Are you okay? Where is he keeping you? Did you get away?"

"Oh Sis, you're so dramatic. I'm *fine*. I've always been fine."

I shook my head, feeling tears sting my eyes. "You haven't been using?"

A pause. "I can handle myself."

Some of my worry came out as anger. I preferred it that way. "And I suppose you can handle Dmitri too?"

"Of course." She giggled in a flirty way that told me Dmitri was right beside her. "He's a *man*, Della. You know as well as I do how to handle them."

Yeah, I had believed I could handle men. Men like Dmitri. Dancing at his club until I could figure out something better, something safer. Except he hadn't wanted to let me go. He hadn't wanted to let Caro go either, and she hadn't put up a fight. Even when he had contacted me with his horrible proposition, I'd thought I could handle him. Give him what he wanted so he'd leave my sister alone.

But this entire thing was getting out of hand.

"Put Dmitri on the phone," I said.

"I thought you didn't like him," she said with a smirk in her voice. "You said you weren't going to talk to him and neither should I."

"And look how well that turned out," I snapped. I forced myself to calm. It wasn't Caro's fault. She didn't understand. I had to believe that, because the alternative, thinking that Caro really wanted a man as thoroughly disgusting as that, made me hate my sister. Dmitri was the scum of the earth. He was the dirt underneath my bare feet. "I have some business with him."

Caro made a dismissive sound. "You with your job. Working crazy hours, and for what? Fifty K a year?"

Less, but I wasn't about to tell her that. "Some of us have bills to pay."

"And you wonder why I stick with Dmitri. No rent, no electricity or whatever the fuck. It's just a good time, okay? So stop being a downer." There was rustling, and her voice became muted. "She wants to talk to you."

In the pause, I knew the phone had been passed to Dmitri. Even the energy over the airwaves felt different. Or maybe the difference was inside me—tension and fear. I hated being afraid of him.

"Hello, love," he said in that oily way of his.

"Let my sister go," I said without preamble.

He laughed. "She doesn't want to leave. You heard her. I treat her very well."

"All the crack she wants, right?"

"Of course not. That stuff is expensive. I don't waste more than I have to on a dirty whore."

"I hope she heard you," I hissed.

"You know me better than that," he said mildly, and he was right.

I knew exactly how careful he could be. He hadn't started working with that international cartel by accident. His brutal reputation had preceded him. He was known widely for despicable acts against both the criminals he worked with and the innocent people around them. Acts like this one.

"Do you have the package?" he asked.

I rolled my eyes. "You mean the human being you asked me to sentence to death?"

"Caro was right, you *are* dramatic. You aren't sentencing anyone to death. That's my job."

"What does that make me, the mailman? No, thank you."

"Are you trying to defy me, sweetheart? We both know that doesn't work out well. For you, for me. For your sister."

"If you hurt a single hair on her head—"

"I won't start with her hair. No, that wouldn't do. Her fingers would be the best place. Those pretty nails she keeps painted because she thinks I'll keep fucking her if she does. I'll take a pair of pliers and tear each one out of the soft skin, one by one."

"Stop." I felt sick. The images were all too real in my mind. Other girls who'd disappeared for weeks. Their bodies were found later in a back alley or in the river. The police would come around with pictures of them from the morgue, their eyes dull and lifeless.

*Do you know her?* they would ask.

*Sure, I saw her around. She danced here too. But we weren't close. No, I don't know who killed her. She didn't have any enemies.*

Lies. Dmitri was our common enemy. As soon as we stepped out of line, we'd end up like them. Everyone knew it. Even the police knew it, after a while, but they still couldn't stop him. Powerless and small, I couldn't stop him either—but I *would* keep my sister safe.

"Please, leave Caro alone. She hasn't done anything to you. Let her go, and I'll take her place. I'll come and do…" I swallowed hard. "Whatever you want."

There was a weighted pause. "What an offer, sweetheart. You've managed to surprise me. I can't say it's not tempting. Unfortunately, business is business, and I need that passenger. Please tell me you're going to deliver him soon."

"I couldn't—" I scrambled to think of a believable excuse, something that would keep Dmitri from storming my house tonight but wouldn't piss him off enough to hurt Caro. "He asked me out on a date, though. I'm seeing him tomorrow. I'll get him then."

"Where is he now?" Dmitri sounded cross.

Why did Dmitri want this guy so badly? "He went to stay with a buddy of his. From the military. And by the way, it really would have helped if you had told me about that."

It felt like a sick joke, like getting some kind of guardian angel sent down to help me, my own person G. I. Joe. But helping me was the last thing he would do if he knew the truth about me. And no matter how strong or how fierce, no single man could go up against Dmitri's resources and win.

"What does it matter? He is a man, yes? You know what to do with them." His voice was mocking me, not only from Caro's words earlier but also all the times he had seen me onstage. Back then he'd been the owner of a strip club that dealt in drugs, and then guns, out of the back rooms. Oh, and flesh. He'd pull any of the girls back there if a customer flashed the right amount of money. The first time it had happened to me, I'd fought the asshole customer. And lost.

Then I'd paid the price when Dmitri taught me a lesson afterward.

"You're despicable," I said through gritted teeth.

"Yes," he said amicably. "Which is all the more reason for you to give me what I want. Someone is going to die tomorrow. I'd prefer it was your new boyfriend. But if he's not here… if I'm very angry… there's a young woman in my bed as we speak, just waiting for me to wrap my hands around her neck."

"Don't touch her!"

The hollow sound of his laughter sent chills down my spine. Then the line went dead. I stared at the screen of my phone until the backlight went off. A second later it dinged with an incoming text. There was an address from the same unlisted number as the call. Fabulous.

I had the package. I had the destination. So why couldn't I make the delivery?

*Because an innocent man will die.* But I'd stopped believing in innocence a long time ago. I didn't really care that he was innocent, that he fought for his country, that he probably helped little old ladies across the street like a goddamned Boy Scout. The truth was, I didn't want him to die because I liked him. Really liked him. And that was the kind of mistake that could get me killed.

# CHAPTER SIX

## CLINT

I WOKE UP to the smell of pancakes and bacon. My stomach grumbled and rolled, a little earthquake underneath my abs. I hadn't eaten much on the flight from Germany. Before that it had been hospital food while they dug shrapnel out of my arm. And before that it had been knockoff MREs. Not even the regular nutrient-dense stuff the army had; this was cheap imitation they served security personnel at the warehouse where I'd been undercover.

In short, I was fucking ravenous.

But I made a pit stop in the bathroom and grabbed a hot shower, determined to feel human again. Besides, Della had invited me into her room—the least I could do was not look like a slob.

I found her in the kitchen, sunlight streaming through the propped-open window above the sink. Her blonde hair was pale gold, limned with light. She looked like a goddamned angel, and for the first time I wondered if I really did need to hook up with one of the military's counselors. But if Della were some PTSD-induced delusion, I didn't really want to know.

My training had taught me to move lightly, all two hundred and sixty pounds of me, so I shuffled on purpose so as not to scare her.

She turned to look at me, and her smile nearly stopped my heart. *Mercy.* My hand actually went to my chest and rubbed absently, trying to relieve the ache.

"Hey, soldier," she said with that Southern twang that drove me crazy. "How'd you sleep?"

"Like a log. Thanks again for letting me stay the night."

Something flickered in her expression. "You're welcome to stay as long as you need."

Damn, I wanted to stay for a long time. But there was a hesitation in her voice that told me she wasn't comfortable with the idea.

"Don't worry about it. I'm going to call up my buddy from the plane. Maybe crash on his couch." Even though I felt bad for interrupting James's reunion, I was running low on options. And though he might grumble, I knew he wouldn't leave me hanging. We'd been through hell and back together.

"No! Please stay." Her expression smoothed out. Her eyes filled with sensual light. "I'll make it worth your while."

I studied her. This girl was throwing off mixed signals like crazy. Her words and actions had been nothing but welcoming. And I sure as hell wanted her—more than her bed, I wanted her body. I wanted all of her. I just couldn't ignore the shadows in her eyes. It was clear my presence here was making her uncomfortable, so I should leave. Today.

And hope she'd agree to meet me for a date after that.

"Look, Della. You're a beautiful girl." She looked alarmed, but I was done wondering where we stood. At least she'd know how I felt about her. "I know we just met, but I really like you. I want to keep seeing you after this."

"Keep seeing me after...?" She seemed cautious. What had made her so cautious?

"I want to take you out. Be with you. I'm not asking for a commitment, but I'd at least like to see where it goes. You mean more to me than a place to crash."

Emotion washed over her face, faster and more riotous than I could read. She turned back to the stove and flipped a pancake. She was withdrawing from me, but I let her go. If there was one thing I'd learned in my life, it was to ask for what I wanted, and I wanted her. But I wouldn't push her either. I'd put my offer on the table. Now it was up to her to accept it or tell me to go.

"Sit down," she said, her voice muffled. She didn't turn or look at me as she bustled to pull plates down. "Breakfast is ready."

I could be obedient when I had to be. In order to get pancakes, for example. And these weren't ordinary pancakes. She placed a plate in front of me loaded with a full stack, diced peaches, and cream that looked loose enough to be hand whipped. On a side plate were two eggs sunny-side up and two strips of glistening bacon.

"Mercy," I muttered.

She smiled, and the corners of her eyes crinkled, letting me know this one was real. "Figured you'd be hungry."

"Starving." I waited until she'd gotten a plate with a single pancake and a side of scrambled eggs before eating. I slathered the pancakes with warm maple syrup until they were heavy and thick.

The first bite was pure sex on a fork, and I couldn't stop the groan that came out of me. My eyes met hers, and heat sparked between us. Jesus God, she was going to be the death of me. I cut another bite—three pancakes deep—and made sure to grab peaches and whipped cream this time. *Even better.*

"You like it?" she asked, a half smile playing at her lips.

The little minx. "I wasn't planning on rushing you, I swear, but I gotta know... will you marry me?"

She laughed, the sound lighting up the air around us like glimmers in twilight. I wanted to make her laugh over and over, until those shadows never entered her eyes again.

Her expression dimmed. "You really should know more about a girl before you ask questions like that."

Yeah, that was true enough. I had always been quick to fall for girls. I looked big and tough, so they figured they could jerk me around and I wouldn't get hurt. And sure, I had muscles. Moving shit, I could handle. But getting cheated on and lied to... that kind of stuff ate away at me.

"Why did you pick me up?" I asked.

For a second she looked stricken. Then she smiled, a dark, wicked grin that made my body heat. "Because I have plans for you, soldier."

Yes, ma'am.

I focused on eating the delicious breakfast she'd made, finishing off my plate and swiping the rest of the bacon right off the pan. She ate a quarter of her pancake and a whole cup of tea, making me wonder if she worked at keeping her slender figure so she could move through the aisle easily.

Or maybe she just liked looking that way. I sure as hell liked how she looked, but it had nothing to do with the circumference of her waist. She was sexy as hell—her curves, her hollows, and everything in between.

Even her eyes were sexy, the thick lashes and knowing glint. She moved with an effortless seduction…and I remembered what James had said about her walking like a stripper. Everything in her house spoke of wholesome Southern charm, but her innate sensuality… those shadows in her eyes…

"What did you do before you were a stewardess?"

Her eyebrows rose. "Picked up guys at bars, I guess. Grocery stores. The usual places."

"Nice deflection."

She shrugged.

And normally I'd let it go. It wasn't my style to pry, especially in this situation with a beautiful woman who was setting her boundaries. But it felt like some crucial piece of the puzzle, the cinch in the middle when I'd only begun to work at the edges.

"Seriously," I pushed as gently as I could.

She ran her fingertip over the top of her cup, swirling once, twice, and my body tightened. Her gaze met mine. "Fine, you caught me. I've never picked up a guy before you. They always came to me. After work." Her laugh was hollow. "Before work. During work."

My stomach clenched, imagining all those guys hitting on her. Not taking no for an answer? Those fucking shadows in her eyes. "Sounds rough," was all I said.

Her expression twisted into something like a smile but far too painful to be one. "I was a stripper, Clint. And whatever else they wanted me to be. Okay?"

She stood abruptly, her chair scraping against the hardwood floors. Her hands were shaking as she gathered her cup and the plates and went to the sink. I sat there, processing. I supposed it shouldn't have been a surprise. It wasn't, really. James was pretty fucking perceptive when he wanted to be. So, she was a stripper.

And whatever else they wanted her to be.

I could guess what that was. I could also guess how horrible it must have been for her. Her pain and humiliation filled the air in the small, sunlit kitchen. My fists were clenched, imagining whatever asshole had made her feel this way. People probably figured a soldier would be violent, but not me. I'd rather keep things calm and avoid a fight—no one had to get hurt. But right now, if that guy was in front of me, I'd pound him into the floor. Over and over again until his face was so disfigured everyone would know he was a monster inside as well as out.

The water ran and dishes clinked, and I knew I was hiding from her. Keeping my reaction in check as I remained at the table. She had retreated, but now I was retreating in my own way.

I followed her to the sink.

Her body tensed, telling me in clear terms to stay away. She was used to shutting guys out. I should respect that, but I also knew that staying away from her now would be the greatest insult. She'd take it as a rejection—which was clearly all she expected. She'd spit out the truth of her past and thought I would judge her for it.

I rested my hands lightly on her hips, giving her time to pull away or tell me no. She stayed very still, not moving. The only sound in the room was the rushing from the faucet. By slow degrees, the tension in her body changed from fear to awareness.

"You okay?" I asked softly.

"Why?" she asked bitterly. "Looking for a private dance?"

"You don't have to do anything you don't want to."

She laughed bitterly. "That's where you're wrong, soldier."

God, she was a contradiction. She invited me in and then glared at me for being there. I couldn't figure it out. Maybe I didn't want to figure it out. That would mean acknowledging that I should leave her alone.

I didn't want to leave her alone.

She felt so warm in my hands, so slender and supple. I kept remembering her mouth on me—glorious, hot—and I desperately wanted to return the favor. I couldn't imagine her tasting anything but sweet. That was her, the Georgia peach, splashing on my tongue. But maybe the sugar would be balanced with feminine musk. She turned wary when I least expected it, undertones of earth and darkness to balance out her smile.

"I really should leave," I said, my voice hoarse, my offer desperate and halfhearted.

She turned in my arms. Her eyelids had lowered, the sunlight bathing her face in a sensual glow. "Stay. I'll make it worth your while."

I wanted every wicked thing her husky tone offered, but I wanted even more. I pulled her off balance, so that she tumbled against my chest. Then I held her close, her cheek lined up to my heart, her arms around my waist. Something shifted inside me and locked into place. When she was touching me, holding me, it felt like everything would be okay. Yeah, my cock was hard for her, but I could have stayed like this forever, feeling her breasts rise and fall, arms wrapped around her strong and vulnerable body.

She took my hand and led me back to the bedroom. I knew it was a power play, a way for her to regain control of the situation, and I let her do it. When she snapped at me to undress, I obeyed her again. I would have followed her to the ends of the earth in that moment—and fallen right off the sepia waterfall like one of those old-time maps.

I stood there, naked, with my hard-on thick and heavy in front of me. My cock had been at half-mast since I woke up, knowing I was in Della's house, hoping I'd get to fuck her today. That blowjob had been so amazing and so cruel all at once, giving me endless pleasure without a drop of hers.

"Get on the bed," she ordered.

I gave her a sideways glance. Her expression remained stern and unyielding, and my body responded with a predictable tightening. I'd always had a thing for powerful women.

"Face up or face down?" I asked mildly.

She had expected me to refuse. Now her surprise had nowhere to go. "Face up," she murmured. "I want to see that beautiful cock pointing at the ceiling."

*That beautiful cock* definitely liked the idea of being watched by her. It throbbed with painful arousal as I climbed onto the bed and lay on my back. My time in the army had demolished any sense of modesty I might have had. Even before then, in foster homes, we were typically operating with too many kids to a bathroom. I didn't get embarrassed. I wasn't scandalized to have flashed my bare ass to a woman I didn't know well. Except when I turned to look at her, the heated approval in her eyes warmed me from the inside out, turning my blood to molten desire and making my cheeks flush.

She smiled. "You like this."

I grunted my assent.

"No, I mean, you really like this. Being told what to do in bed."

The thought jolted me more than her command had done. Did I like being told what to do? Probably any military guy had a bit of a masochist in him. Physical training could be brutal, and the political maneuvers and mind games were even worse. But that was my professional life. Not my sex life.

Slowly shaking my head, I said, "I like being with you. I'm not too particular on how we do it."

Her grin was knowing. "Whatever you say. It just so happens that I *am* particular, so you won't mind if I run things, will you?"

I snorted. Oh yeah, she could control me six ways to Sunday. "Whatever you say," I repeated.

Her eyes flashed with pleasure. I thought she shivered, even though she had on her clothes—unlike me. But then she straightened, reverting to the aloof vibe I didn't buy for a second. She crossed the room and climbed onto the bed beside me. My cock perked up, pointing to the ceiling exactly as she'd ordered it to.

Neat trick. I wondered what else she could make me do.

Her nails scored over my thigh, abrasive and ticklish all at once. I tensed. She pushed my thighs apart, and after the briefest hesitation—Jesus, this was hot—I spread my legs. Kneeling between them, she propped her chin on her fist and examined me. I felt like an object. An interesting, beautiful object. A zing of desire traveled straight down my cock and into my balls.

She tapped her chin. "Let's see what we're working with here."

We would be working with a spent cock if she kept looking at me that way. My body was ready to explode and she hadn't even touched me yet. It came to me then, how dangerous she could be. Great sex was one thing. Falling for a girl was something else. Both at the same time might be the blow from which I wouldn't recover.

Her forefingers lined up on either side of my cock, running from the base to the flared head. There may as well have been a ruler in her hands. The little smile on her face didn't let me feel too nervous about how I measured up. Her fingers slid back down, dragging the skin, making me gasp at the sensation, flesh pulled taut and exposed. Then her thumb brushed right over the tip.

"Ahh, God. Not there. Not yet." My body trembled with the force it took to stay still and flat on the bed.

"Did I touch a nerve?" she asked with feigned innocence.

"Every single one," I muttered.

She laughed. "I like your honesty."

Hmm, who appreciated honesty? People who had been lied to. Or people who were lying. I filed that away for future consideration.

"Honestly, I want to see your body. I want to touch you." The words came out hoarse, but I didn't care. The throbbing erection between us already gave away how much I wanted her.

Her gaze was considering. "All right, soldier. Let's play a game."

My stomach sank. Why did I get the impression I wasn't going to like this? *Or maybe I'd like it too much?*

"The game works like this. I'll ask you a question. For every one you get right, I'll take off an article of my clothing. Whatever you see, you can touch."

"And if I get it wrong?"

Her hand grabbed my balls before I could slam my legs shut. She twisted, and I jerked against her—then froze. Though she wasn't squeezing tight enough to injure me, I was definitely sweating the pressure. If she *had* been really hurting me, I could have dislodged her. There were a hundred ways to do so. But I wouldn't risk her getting hurt. And more importantly, I wanted to play this game. *Whatever you can see, you can touch.* Hunger was a fierce ache in my gut, to see all of her, to touch her everywhere.

"If you get it wrong," she said mildly, "then you get punished. You're in the military. I'm sure you're used to punishments."

She hadn't released the vice on my balls, and I was panting now. "Sure, I can scrub the floor by hand if you want."

"That's not a bad idea." Her eyes sparkled with wicked intent. "Bent over and naked. It's a very vulnerable position. It'd give me great access to your ass."

*Jesus.* My heart rate kicked into double time. What

was she going to do with my ass? "Uh—"

"Shhh, don't worry about that. Because I know you're going to be a very good boy, aren't you?"

I swallowed hard. "Yes, ma'am."

As if those were the magic words, she released me. I slumped back onto the bed, relieved and massively turned on. Unnaturally turned on, as if she had sprinkled pixie dust on my overdue cock. A blowjob—even a glorious one—wasn't going to cut it. I needed a long, hard fuck. And then I needed to do it again, and again, until we were both slippery and sated and blissed out on pleasure.

"First question. This one has three parts—name, rank, and serial number."

Surprise ran a live wire through my body, but I managed to hide the worst of my reaction. It was like getting kicked in the gut and falling back into three weeks ago, neck-deep in the cartel, under constant threat of discovery and torture.

I told myself she had just seen too many action flicks. This was her way of getting to know me. Or maybe she just wanted a little rough play in the bedroom. Okay, judging from the way she twisted my balls, a lot of rough play.

"Clint Adams. Specialist." I rattled off my serial number, ignoring the twinge of unease. This was hardly confidential information. Any old girlfriend would have had access to that information if she'd looked at my papers. Of course, Della wasn't my girlfriend.

And there was too much intent in her eyes for me to

write off her interest as random curiosity.

"Your turn," I said gruffly. "Pay up. Let me see you, sweet girl."

With a smirk, she slipped off her socks. "Here you go."

The little cheat. I gestured with my hand. "Pay up. Let me feel them."

Her gaze turned worried. "You aren't going to tickle me, are you?"

"Of course not." I waited until she sat scooted sideways and slid her foot into my palm before adding, "Unless I don't like your question."

She tried to yank her foot away, but I wouldn't let her. Her stern expression didn't fool me. I wanted to kiss the little line between her eyebrows, smooth away the stress on her forehead. I wanted to shove my fingers inside her pussy and rub her clit until the only expression on her face was rapture.

I couldn't touch that part of her, though. Only her feet.

So I focused on them, tugging her so that she was fully reclined, both her feet in my hands. They were small feet, delicate feet to match the rest of her body. Still, I knew how much she must stand on them with her job.

I pressed hard against the insole with my thumb, thoroughly enjoying the soft moan she emitted. I took it as a challenge and caressed her foot from the tips of her toes to the curve of her heel, teasing out more sexy sounds.

"Enough," she gasped, and I wanted to argue. I wasn't nearly done with her feet, but I wanted to see other parts more, so I released her.

She struggled to get her composure back, and I did nothing to help her. Seeing her primly walking down the aisle had turned my crank, but watching her eyes roll back and those plush lips part—yeah, I was getting more of that. Even if it meant playing by her rules. Even if it meant breaking them.

"Next question?" I prodded.

"How...how long? How long have you been in the military?"

Shit, another probing question? She chose that moment to probe me—literally—in the shadowed cleft beneath my balls. I strung up tight and let out a strangled sound. *She's distracting you.* Protective instincts knew what was up, but god-fucking-damn it, she was really good at distraction. Really good when her forefinger teased the puckered hole, threatening to push inside but pulling back instead. I didn't know if the tightness in my chest was relief or disappointment.

"Three years," I ground out.

Her next question came immediately. "And before then?"

"Two items." Only when she sighed and nodded did I say, "Before that I graduated high school. Foster parents asked me to leave since they weren't getting money anymore, so I enlisted. Been there ever since."

She nodded as if I'd confirmed something she suspected. I didn't want to think about what that might be, so I tugged on the soft, stretchy hem of her shirt. "Off."

"Ooh, so you do know how to give orders." She winked, and I made a low growling sound I hadn't even known I was capable of. Sure, I'd ordered a girl around before. I'd spanked her ass before, but only if she asked for it first. Sex had always been a respectful and obliging sort of exercise—one that ended in an orgasm, so who was complaining?

She pulled off her shirt, exposing the pale expanse of her chest and abdomen. A black lace bra covered her breasts, though it enhanced rather than restricted my view.

I waited with my breath locked up tight. *Reach back, undo the clasp.* "Let me see those pretty tits," I gasped.

She grinned. "I love how eager you are."

So of course she did the opposite thing. Of course she wiggled on the bed and scooted out of her denim shorts, revealing a matching pair of black panties that made my mouth water. The glimpse of her ass made my fingers twitch to touch it—and I could now. I could run my hands along legs that went on and on.

Her skin was like silk and the edges of her lace panties as rough as sandpaper. The contrast made me greedy. I slipped two fingers underneath the hem, wanting more, needing her, and she dug her nails in where my thigh met my groin.

"Bad," she said imperiously. It might as well have been a rolled-up newspaper slapped on my nose.

Humiliation warred with arousal. Goose bumps

spread over my skin like wildfire, like rain. I was alternately set ablaze and then doused, left chilled and damp and ready to begin again.

With Della, sex became a battle. She fought for every inch and set up barricades around herself so that I'd have to fight too. She drew out every combat instinct I had learned over the past three years—and before that. In the system, you learned early on about simple brute force, about bullies who would beat you up just because they could. I could overpower Della with a twist of my wrist, but I didn't want that. I wanted to do what I did on an op: infiltrate her defenses and strike when she least expected it.

"God, Della," I groaned. "Give me more."

"Then earn it, big boy."

"Ask me a fucking question," I demanded. Anger pulsed in my erection, hungry and dangerous. I wanted her to refuse just so I could go over the edge. What would happen next? In every other situation I would back down, I would do what she wanted, but this wasn't every other situation. Della wasn't like other women I'd been with. It was almost like she wanted me to get mad at her, and my dick was happy to oblige.

She pulled back at the last minute. I imagined the doctor trembling at this moment, afraid of the monster he had created. Pretending she still had control in the form of a question. "What did you do there? The place you just came from? What did you *do?*"

Jesus fuck, what did I do? I killed people, that's what I

did. I shot them or slit their throats or choked the life out of them. Is that what she wanted to hear? Is that what she got off on?

The op had been messy as hell and no less bloody than a battlefield, but we'd won. Almost a million dollars in arms confiscated on its way into the US and twenty of their men currently in custody. As for the rest, they were going to turn their remaining guns on each other in the age-old blame game. So why did she fucking care?

"I did my job," I said, reaching for the scrap of lace that connected her bra in the front.

She jerked out of reach. "Not good enough."

"It's the fucking truth. Those were the rules of the game." It was almost an out-of-body experience as I launched myself after her and grappled her onto the bed. I never did stuff like this. I would never hurt a woman, but she winced before I loosened my grip on her wrists.

She panted beneath me, her eyes shooting sparks. "The rules are whatever I say they are. And that answer wasn't good enough."

I snarled—that was the sound that came out of me. She was a witch who had turned me into an animal. I would howl at the moon and stamp my paw in frustration. My dick hung heavy beneath me, bobbing, aching to be inside her. I could nudge her legs apart and push in. I could feel her hot warmth around me even with her shouting no.

She wouldn't say no.

I tightened my grip on her arms, fury running through my body like a physical pain. "Do you want me to share classified information to play your fuckin' game? Do I have to violate national security just to fuck you?"

"So what if you do?" she asked, her voice haughty and breathless.

Reaching behind her, I yanked at the clasp on her bra. No finesse, just power. I heard the sound of metal snapping and stretching as the hooks came undone. The straps cut into her arms, leaving white lashes down her skin that faded by the time I threw the bra across the room. She didn't fight me, even though I broke the rules. Or maybe she just knew me well enough, even in this short amount of time, to know I would follow them after all.

"I infiltrated a criminal organization, an international arms dealer." That was for the bra. I pushed my fingers into the front hem of her panties and squeezed my fist tight. When I pulled my arm back, the lace came with it. Now I owed her another belated answer, so I gave her the next logical step. I gave her details. "They were in Russia. I was in Russia until two weeks ago. We brought down the organization, their shipping channels. We took their supplies and froze their accounts. They're dead in the water."

Her eyes widened, but I was too far gone to think about how a civilian might be afraid. I was too pissed off to care if she wanted to back out. She was naked now, but even without clothes she was only a blur. Pink and cream and a strip of blonde hair down her sex. I plunged two fingers inside her pussy, rough and vengeful.

"I didn't—" She looked stricken.

"You didn't say I could touch you here? Why, because I can't see it? Deep inside where you're so wet and swollen for me, I can't see it, but I can feel it."

Her eyes were wide. "I didn't mean to hurt you."

I laughed, the sound hollow and mournful in my chest. "You didn't hurt me." God, she was so slender beneath me, so fragile. "You *can't* hurt me."

"Clint, stop. You aren't like this. This isn't you."

I'd never disagreed with her more. In that moment I could only see her skin and the blood of my enemies. I could only see rare moments of kindness and senseless violence. I lived on this line every goddamned day. This was my life. This was *me*.

"I tell you what, sweetheart. I'll give you one more answer for free, before I fuck this pretty pussy of yours." I twisted my fingers inside her, rubbing the pad along her wall until she cried out. I wasn't sure she could even hear me anymore, and maybe that was for the best. "What I said before, that's only what the US government knows about. There's something else, something they don't want to know about, something no one can know about."

"What?" Her eyes were glazed, and I brushed my thumb over her clit to make it worse.

"That's right. It's dangerous and it's technically illegal and it's mine. That's who you're fucking right now. A goddamned traitor."

Even though I had done it for the good of the country, that was what I'd be labeled if shit went south. The list could start an international conflict that would mean more bloodshed. My commander was bound by a million and one restrictions not to act on that list, not to even acknowledge its existence. The only person who knew I had this list was James. I would figure out some way to get the list into the hands of the right officials.

Of course, it was supposed to be a secret.

It pissed me off that I had confided in this woman, that I'd let her lead me around by my dick. It pissed me off that she pried into things she shouldn't know about, shouldn't care about. It pissed me off that she kept secrets from me. So I made her pay for it by pushing inside her without any warning, by stretching the walls of her pussy with my cock until she gasped and clenched and shuddered in my arms.

"Clint. Oh, *Clint*." Jesus, she sounded sad. It made me want to hide her away and cheer her up. It made me want to drag her to my cave and dress her in furs. I settled for giving her an orgasm, angling my cock to hit that spot that made her moan.

I thrust inside her, my hips pistoning like mad. Her hot flesh wrapped around me like leather pulling tight. That was how I saw her: dark and slick and rising from the ashes. So wet without any barriers—no condom. *Shit.* But she couldn't have pushed me away at the moment. Nothing could have torn my cock from her thirsty, gripping cunt except her soft cries of ecstasy. Even then I kept going, grunting on every downstroke—harder, deeper, around the moon and back again. I managed to pull out right before I came in a splash on her belly, come pooling in her navel, creamy and white, a milky reflection of all that I'd lost.

# CHAPTER SEVEN
## DELLA

THIS WAS BAD. Very bad.

If last night's blowjob had been a mistake, the amazing sex today was a disaster. I couldn't stop thinking about what Dmitri would do to him. All I had were whispers, gossip that had passed through the back room at the club. Fingers cut off. Burn marks. Torture.

I had managed to forget all that when it was only my sister's life on the line. After all, whatever Dmitri would do to a man, he would do worse to a woman. Before I'd gotten on that plane, I'd known the deal.

Bring the passenger in seat 34B, and my sister would be released, safe and sound.

"You okay?"

I jumped. The previous passenger of 34B was looking at me with concern. And he was holding a hammer. The door to the garage was open behind him, giving me a clue as to where he'd gotten it from—his own boxes. I just didn't know why.

"Uh... what're you doing with that?" I asked.

He hefted the tool in his hand. "Figured I'd check out that loose step on your front porch."

My eyebrows shot up. "My what?"

I had expected him to check something out, but not my loose step. *Isn't this what you wanted?* This way, I wouldn't have to have sex with him again. And I could be assured that he would stay for a while. But the problem was… I kind of wanted to have sex with him again, right the fuck now. Earlier had only been a taste. Through some combination of sympathy and ordinary lust, I wanted this man in my bed.

The other problem was I wasn't sure I wanted him to stay anymore. If he stayed, Dmitri would get him. If he stayed with me, he was going to die.

"You mind?" he asked. At my confused look, he added, "If I check out your step."

I shrugged. "Suit yourself."

He headed onto the porch with a rusted red toolbox. I followed, too intrigued to ignore what he was doing. And what *was* he doing? Paying his way? Looking after me? I didn't know what it meant that he'd noticed a problem in my life and decided to fix it. But it filled me with a strange and unfamiliar warmth.

Or maybe that was just lust. His ass did look amazing in those jeans as he knelt to examine the steps.

"You find the problem, doctor?" I asked.

He glanced back and smiled. "Nothing a little nailing won't fix."

I laughed out loud. "You were waiting to say that, weren't you?"

"When you get a chance, you take it. Hang tight. I

gotta grab some of that spare wood I saw in the garage."

He headed around the side of the house, and I watched him go, my smile fading. *When you get a chance, you take it.* That was exactly what I had with him: a chance. It felt like I was holding opportunity in my bare hands, white-hot, burning the skin right off my palms. The calculating part of my brain was telling me to use him like the hammer and nails he held. Nothing but a tool to get my sister back. But I had never been all that analytical. I had wanted all three plants to live in my science experiment. I wanted the same thing here, but instead of three plants there was me, my sister, and Clint. I wanted us all to get out of this alive.

Clint came back around the house with a piece of wood under his arm. "You want to help?"

A wave of shyness washed over me. I had no idea where it came from. I hadn't been shy since I was twelve years. I was forced to get over any sort of modesty then. I gave up my dignity too. But Clint gave a little of it back to me with every gentlemanly gesture.

"What do I have to do?" I asked.

"For starters, this." He tugged me in for a quick kiss. The warm day had already coated him in a thin layer of sweat, and his nose left dampness on my cheek. I wriggled away, pretending to mind. But the truth was I loved the clean-sweat smell of him. I loved that he was making himself useful around the house even though he didn't have to. I loved everything about him, and it was getting harder and harder to pretend he wouldn't hate me if he knew the truth.

He held up the hammer, as if for me to take it. But when I grabbed for it, he pulled it out of my reach.

"Repeat after me," he said in a serious voice. "I promise not to smash Clint's thumb."

I rolled my eyes but complied. "I promise not to smash Clint's thumb."

He let me grab the hammer's handle, but he didn't release the other end. His gaze met mine. "And I promise to make more of my amazing pancakes for Clint tomorrow."

My breath caught. If I did what I promised Dmitri, Clint shouldn't even be here tomorrow. I should turn him over tonight. I had to force the words out, and even then, they only came out as a whisper. "I promise to make more of my amazing pancakes for Clint tomorrow."

How could I keep that promise when my sister needed me?

Instead of relinquishing the hammer, Clint used it to pull me close. I fell against him, my free hand landing on his broad chest. God, he was so solid. I leaned into him and breathed deep. Would I remember his scent long after he was gone? That thought hurt my heart.

But the thought that I might forget hurt worse.

Clint's gaze was faintly knowing. "I promise to tell Clint if I'm in trouble."

My eyes widened. I released the hammer and stepped back. How did he know I was in trouble? "What?"

He sighed, looking aggravated and guilty at the same

time. He ran a hand over his hair, cut military short. "Sorry. I pushed too far?"

"I have no idea what you're talking about," I lied.

Those soft eyes asked me to open up. "If something's wrong, if someone's hurting you, maybe I can help."

Acid burned me up inside. Oh, he could help, all right. He was my sister's ticket to freedom, only it meant he'd end up hurt. End up dead. That wasn't supposed to matter to me. I'd seen enough people pass through my life not to care. Only Caro should matter anymore.

"I don't want your help," I said too sharply. Because it was true. I didn't want him to help with this.

I wanted him to be safe.

He sighed but didn't push. When he handed me the hammer this time, there were no more demands, no more empty promises. He positioned the board and held the nail in place.

"Go ahead," he said, nodding toward the nail.

I bent down and lined up the hammer. Then with a careful, firm swing I landed the hammer directly on the nail. I didn't smash his thumb, because at least this promise I could keep.

He took over the rest of the work while I watched from a few feet away. His body gleamed in the sunlight, sweat dripping down his neck, his arms. His body was a contrast of beauty and roughness, of taut muscles and fading bruises he must have gotten overseas. He'd been beaten and shot at over there, but he probably felt safe back on American soil. Only, he wasn't.

I had to look away. I blinked into the sunlight, which streamed through the tree above me and around the roof of my house. The Victorian was old and falling down in parts, and I couldn't love it more. When things broke, I patched it up the best I could. I had been been struggling to save up money, but it wasn't nearly enough to hire contractors or even handymen.

*That's it.* The money. I wondered how much it would take to buy Dmitri off.

Immediately I dismissed that as the stupidest idea I'd ever had. No amount of money was going to keep Dmitri from going after Clint, especially if he knew the guy was staying at my house. And if I waited too long, Dmitri *would* send someone sniffing around and find him here. I couldn't sit around waiting for that to happen.

But what if I showed up and convinced Dmitri that I never got Clint to give me the time of day? I could say the guy went home with a friend from the army. I didn't know who and I didn't know where. At least that would give Clint a fighting chance to get away. And as for getting my sister back… maybe Dmitri would take the money. It wouldn't be the first time I'd had to pay off Caro's debts.

I'd sure as hell rather do it with my life savings than with Clint's life.

I SLEPT UNEASY that night, alternating between glaring at the open bedroom door and squeezing my eyes shut against what I had to do tomorrow. My body was curled into a ball in the center of my bed. Even completely still, I felt dizzy with the weight of my guilt. Whenever I reached out, I found sheets so empty and chilled they left me numb, as if I were floating on a slate of ice with only cold water around me.

There was no one to blame but myself for my current lonely state. I had suggested that we sleep apart tonight, him in his guest room and me in my room. Being the gentleman, he had readily agreed.

I loved and hated that he was a gentleman.

Eventually I slipped into an uneasy dreamscape, a dark and shadowy place in my subconscious. There was a large city with gold pavement and emerald walls. And fire, angry and wild in front of me. Dmitri's slimy voice boomed around me, demanding the broom of passenger 34B as payment so I could return home. But all I found in the witch's fortress was Clint wearing that crooked smile of his. And when I returned to the Emerald City, when I pulled back the curtain—

I woke up in bed, drenched with sweat and panting. My heart beat a million times a minute as I tried to calm down.

The dream had been stupid and obvious, but it managed to solidify my feelings on the matter. I wasn't going to bring Clint to Dmitri. I wasn't going to watch him melt as if he were some kind of witch, because he wasn't. That was the most fucked-up part of all, how sweet he was. How trusting, even though he'd clearly seen the worst humanity had to offer. I'd seen the same things, only I knew better than to trust strangers, even if they had a pretty smile and a white house with a wraparound porch.

Monsters came in all shapes and sizes. They wore custom designer suits and stewardess uniforms. They gave you a job as a stripper or went down on you to help you sleep, but those were just part of the lure. Because when you had learned to trust the monster, when you let your guard down, that's when you got eaten.

When I woke up again, it was morning.

Sun streamed through my white sheer curtains, and birds sang outside my window. I had loved the quaintness of the house when I first moved in. It had felt like a memory I'd never had, a chance to rewrite history. Only now the sweet, homey feeling felt perverse, even grotesque. The universe knew exactly how little I deserved this kind of life. No wonder it had all gone to hell.

I got ready quickly, throwing on a pale blue polka-dot sundress because it was easy. My hair went up into a quick bun, because the last thing I wanted to do was give Dmitri the impression I had primped for him. My task today would be awful, and I'd rather get it over with.

The sizzle and scent of bacon drew me downstairs.

Clint stood in the kitchen wearing worn-looking jeans that hugged his ass, a loose army-green T-shirt, and bare feet. Two white straps wrapped around his waist and tied at the back.

I recognized my apron and let out a startled laugh.

"Hey, Martha Stewart."

He turned back, grinning, pretending to be offended. Then he saw me, and his smile faded. He stayed like that, spatula in hand, eyes on my face, lips pressed together. *Shit.* My heart stalled in my chest. I heard it from beneath the floorboards instead, the telltale heart, and I wanted to blurt out all my sins.

He saved me from doing so, by saying, "You look really good."

My hand went to my falling-down hair in a self-conscious movement. "I'm a mess and you know it."

He shook his head, wearing a half grin that seemed more bemused than anything. As if *I* were the one missing something. His gaze was considering. "Every time I look at you, I see a new side of you." His face screwed into a deprecating expression, as if he knew exactly how cheesy his words were—but couldn't help himself anyway. "Every time, I think you can't look any prettier than that, but then you do."

I blushed like a maniac, my cheeks burning so hot I had to look away. This was flirting, the way I tried to hide my smile and failed. These were practiced movements I had learned a long time ago. I had used them on countless customers and—to my eternal shame—on Dmitri, once upon a time. But they had never come out naturally. I'd never understood *why* a girl would twirl her hair on her finger or bite her lip, until now. It felt as natural as breathing to flirt this way, to scoot closer while huddling in on myself.

"You hungry?" he asked in a low voice, and I knew he wasn't talking about food. The tension pulsed in the room, igniting my desire and alerting me to his. Normally that would be a scary situation. Something to worry about or something that would pay my bills.

Now I wanted to push him up against the counter so he had nowhere to go. I wanted to yank down those jeans and pull up his shirt—but I'd leave the apron on. I liked things twisted. I wanted a man as strong and capable and fearless as him, but I wanted him at my feet.

"I can't stay," I said with genuine regret. "I have some errands to run this morning."

"Oh." He glanced back at the pan of bacon. Scrambled eggs were already split onto two dishes. "You sure I can't tempt you?"

I stuck out my tongue. "You always do."

God, who was this girl? It was like I'd reverted to a sixteen-year-old girl, making faces at guys in the hallway between classes. At least, that was how I guessed it would be. I'd never been to high school, only taken GED courses by mail. I had never been sixteen either—not really. I'd gone from little girl to jaded woman in the blink of an eye.

Clint loaded the bacon and toast onto the plates and brought them to the table. "Just a few minutes," he said. He knew exactly the effect he had on me, the bastard. "You can tell me your plan for the day."

Just like that, all the fun flirtiness evaporated. I did sit down at the table, because walking away from this meal he'd made would be downright criminal. But I couldn't help feeling like this was my last meal. It made the eggs taste rubbery and the bacon like charcoal.

He took a bite but watched me curiously. "The food okay?"

"It's great," I lied.

The sound he made was noncommittal. "Are *you* okay?"

"Of course." I forced a smile. "Just a little tired, I guess."

"Yeah, I guess you have to unwind after all that travel. Jet lag times a thousand."

His voice sounded so sympathetic I actually winced. "It's nothing compared to you. I mean, you were... fighting people. And also traveling. If anyone deserves to relax when you get home, it's you."

Now he looked worried. *About me.* My words had come out too fast, and he knew something was wrong.

"You don't really have to tell me what you have planned for the day," he said quietly. "I'm not going to pry."

My stomach twisted with self-hatred. I wanted the floor to swallow me up. I wanted to die.

He should kill me, really. That was what soldiers did to the enemy—and I was definitely his enemy. What would he do if I told him the truth? I imagined the disbelief on his face, the disillusionment. I imagined his hatred and felt bile rise up in my throat. My fork clattered to the table.

"I really do have to go."

"All right." So fucking agreeable.

He stood when I did, and it pissed me off. "Stop being a gentleman."

His eyebrows shot up. "Pardon me?"

I snorted. "I'm serious. Stop it. It's...annoying."

Was that hurt in his eyes? Great. Someone just shoot me so I could stop being a crazy person, one who kicked puppies and wounded sweet soldiers. Well, odds were good that Dmitri would shoot me today.

"Look," I said. "I'm sorry. Just... do me a favor and don't answer the door while I'm gone. In fact, stay inside, okay? No fixing the porch step until I get back. Got it?"

"Got it," he said, his expression unreadable.

"I'm serious, but I'll be back soon. Like a couple hours at the most." And if I wasn't back by then, there was a decent chance that I wouldn't be back at all. I didn't want to think about what that would look like, but my mind was a heartless bastard. How long would Clint wait here before he figured out I was gone for good? Would he call the police or just leave?

Ugh, now I was planning my own funeral.

I turned to go upstairs and grab my purse. He caught my hand, his fingers ensnaring mine. He wasn't holding me, not forcefully, but I still swung back as if he'd locked me down tight. When I turned to face him, he pressed a kiss to my lips, sweet and questioning. He cared about me. The certainty sank into my bones, building me up in a way I didn't deserve. *Shit.* When had this happened?

Hundreds of passengers, thousands of them, and I had to fall for the one I was supposed to kill.

"See you soon," I forced out, stepping back.

It was only hurry that made me run up the stairs. Not guilt. Not shame that I couldn't even meet his eyes. Not sadness that made me avoid the kitchen when I left the house, not looking for him at all. I walked down the freshly repaired porch step, got into my truck, and drove away. It wouldn't do any good to fall for him. There was no point in dwelling on what might have been. After plotting to kill him, even if I hadn't known him yet, I'd pretty much given up any right to a relationship with him. But I'd try to save him if I could.

I might just die trying.

# CHAPTER EIGHT

## CLINT

**D**ELLA WAS HIDING something. I'd figured that out pretty quickly, but hey, everyone was entitled to their secrets. She'd let me into her home, but she still deserved her privacy.

So I really had no fucking explanation for why I'd stowed away in the bed of Della's truck.

There was a fifteen-minute ride during which I berated myself for being every kind of moron, for being a creepy-ass stalker. She should call the cops on me. This was the behavior that could make the news alongside a special expose on the effects of warfare and PTSD.

And maybe they had a point. I really had to wonder if my head was on straight as I huddled beneath a tarp. Of course following her was wrong, but I'd just seen something in her eyes that I recognized: fear. I needed to find out what—or who—she was afraid of. Even if that made me a nut job. Even if she'd kick me out of her house, and her life, if she knew what I'd done.

The vehicle slowed as she turned into a parking lot. I tensed, wondering where we were. The ambient traffic sounds were the same as they'd been. We hadn't gone too far and we hadn't turned off on any dirt roads. We were off some random city road.

Brakes squeaked as we stopped completely. The window whirred as it rolled down.

"Good morning," said a voice over an intercom. "How can I assist you today?"

The bank. She'd gone to the fucking bank. I raged at myself all over again. *You stalker. You creepy fuck. She let you into her home, she trusted you, and you repay her by following her when she runs legitimate errands.*

"I'd like to check my balance," came Della's voice.

"One moment, please." After a pause, the teller stated a balance of a few hundred bucks in checking and a little over eight thousand dollars in a savings account. Not a bad nest egg. *Creepy. Stalker.*

"I'd like to withdraw eight thousand," she said.

And just like that, the warnings were pinging all over again. Something was wrong here, seriously wrong. Eight thousand bucks in the bank was good stuff for a girl who clearly lived modestly and worked hard. She had a house and a truck. All signs pointed to fiscal responsibility, but she practically runs away from breakfast and withdraws all her money?

No. This girl needed help.

I waited with very little patience while she completed the transaction. I wanted to bust out of the bed of the truck and get some answers. I wanted to demand she let me help her. But that would only terrify her right now. I needed to know more about what I was dealing with. I also needed a little backup.

As we got back on the road, I pulled my cell phone from my pocket and dialed James.

He picked up on the second ring. "Yo."

"Hey, man." Suddenly I felt sheepish. Okay, sure, we told each other everything. But I hadn't forgotten how crazy this made me look. *It looks crazy because it* is *crazy, man.* "How's Rachel?"

"She's good. Better than good. Now why are you calling me from a fucking wind tunnel?"

It was pretty loud in the back of a truck when it was going forty—no, fifty—miles per hour. We had clearly picked up speed, which meant she was heading somewhere else, away from home rather than toward it. Another innocuous errand? Or did she have a plan for her life savings?

"I have a situation," I confessed.

"With the data?" he asked, his voice on high alert.

"No. Shit, no, I haven't even had time to think about that. I've been...distracted."

"Ohh, that kind of distracted."

"Don't say *ohh,* jackass. It's not like that."

"What is it like then?" he asked in a mocking tone, clearly not buying it. As well he shouldn't, since he was on the right track.

"There's this girl." I ignored the smug sound over the phone. "Actually, you know her. Sort of. It's the stewardess from the plane. I needed a ride and then Chelsea kicked me out and—"

"Wait a minute. Chelsea kicked you out? But it was your apartment."

"I know. It's a long story. Well, no, it's not a long story. It's a short one. She asked me to leave and I did. I had no desire to sleep in the bed where she'd fucked another guy."

"Aww, shit."

"Yeah, I know. But Della was there. She'd given me a ride, and I ended up going home with her."

"You fucking dog." Genuine approval rang in his voice.

"Yeah, well. It's been great. She's amazing and I'm more comfortable at her place than I've ever been in my life." *Oh yeah, and I'm falling for her. Hard.*

"So what's with the SOS?"

"I think she's in trouble. She's not telling me much, but the way she looks sometimes…it's like that moment when the shooting starts. You realize there's a very real chance you will die in the next ten minutes, and there's not much you can even do about it. It's just random chance at that point. You think, I've been lucky so far, but maybe it's run out now. That's what I see when I look in her eyes."

"Well, shit. Between the data and this, you sure do know how to find trouble."

It did seem to be an unfortunate trend. And it had all started with that damned data. My commander had wanted me to make the list go away, but I couldn't do that. A split second decision had changed my life. I still didn't regret keeping it. Too many lives could be saved with that information. No matter what fallout happened, I would never regret trying to get it into the right hands, because it was the right thing to do.

"Look," I said. "I don't know what's going down, but I might need your help. I just wanted to let you know."

"Whatever you need, I'm there. You know that."

"Thanks."

I hung up the phone as we pulled onto a gravel road. The truck bounced along the road, and my head slammed into the metal side. "Ouch," I muttered.

Hopefully Della wouldn't have heard that. And wouldn't notice the extra weight she was dragging. She pulled off to the side, rocks crunching beneath her wheels. She stopped the vehicle, and everything went still and silent. Gradually I heard the sound of birds and.... a distant brook. We had definitely left the city and gone into a rural area.

The door opened and closed. Footfalls grew quieter as she walked away.

I counted to sixty before letting myself sit up. *Shit, that hurt.* My neck was cramped from being jolted against metal ridges for a dozen miles. Della was nowhere in sight, but it was clear she'd followed the trail that went through the trees. At some point there was big ranching type of fence that was locked shut, with no call box. She must have stepped between the wooden posts and continued on foot. Behind the truck was only open, empty countryside.

Once assured I was alone, I slipped out of the truck bed and into the trees. From there it was easy to track and catch up to her, moving silently through the brush as she walked along the path. Her head was down. Her posture looked... scared? Defeated?

*Fuck.* Where was she going? She had her purse, which presumably contained the money she'd withdrawn. Was she going to bury it? Was this the ultimate lack of trust in the country's banking system, that she was going to bury her money rather than store it in an account? I wished that was true. It would be a relief to know that she was crazy and not me.

I had come up with half a dozen scenarios for the situation Della was in, and most of them I could handle myself. First on the list was paranoia on my part. Maybe nothing was wrong. Maybe she wasn't afraid. And maybe my PTSD was projecting all over her. That one scared me because of its implications on my sanity. But at least that one would mean Della was safe.

*Safe from everyone except me.*

There were other, more mundane options, like an abusive ex. Just let him try and touch her. I'd beat the ever-loving fuck out of him, and then I'd *really* feel relieved. Neither she nor I would be crazy, and a violent bastard would get what he had coming to him. I wouldn't even call James for anything like that. It would be just one-on-one. I'd show him what it felt like to be hit by someone stronger than him.

But the last option... Jesus, the last option seemed to

be the right one. I had the awful suspicion that I was dealing with something much worse than PTSD, much bigger than an asshole ex-boyfriend. And as I came to the clearing where the woods stopped, I knew that was the right answer.

*Can I take Criminal Hideouts for $500, Alex?*

Yeah, this place was bad news. And Della had gone inside. I wanted to shake her for being so reckless. I wanted to tie her up until she explained how she knew these people and why she'd come here. I had to focus instead on breaking in and hoping their security was god awful. I really wished I'd brought my gun.

THE PLACE WAS way out in the country, but it was clearly built for a rich-ass homeowner. Unlike Della's lush green lawn and flower bed of daisies, this place had neatly trimmed hedges that would rival a castle in freakin' England. The house itself was a sleek modern structure that looked out of place in the countryside. The whole setup screamed *I have money and power. Please someone suck my dick.*

Pathetic.

Two guards stood on either side of the door. They were also pathetic, one half-asleep and the other playing on his phone. I took out the guy on his phone first because he was closer. By the time he had slumped against the wall, unconscious, I had the other guy in a choke hold. He twitched and then went still. I wished I had zip ties to bind their hands, but I had to settle for using their belts in a rough tangle that would come apart when they woke up and worked at it.

But at least I had guns. I tossed the semiautomatic weapons into the hedge nearby and kept both pistols, one in my hand and the other tucked into the back of my jeans. I had no intention of shooting anyone today, but more importantly, I had no intention of getting shot.

*And Della is somewhere inside.*

The place was poorly guarded. Or maybe I was just used to the stringent security protocols we'd used when I was undercover. Part of my role had been a security consultant. Ironically, I'd helped the assholes beef up their security. But since I also knew their routines, their access codes, their procedures, I'd disabled them easily when the time came.

I made it inside the building and saw Della before I heard her. There were several layers of glass between us, as well as an atrium and a garden center beneath oversize vaulted windows. She was talking to some guy in a suit. A guy I immediately wanted to punch, on principle. That was crazy. I was *never* violent.

*PTSD, motherfucker.*

Because now I could have pummeled this guy even without confirming he was an ex-boyfriend, even without knowing he had ever been an abusive one. Just for hugging her and watching her body go tense from twenty feet away.

I slipped closer, still careful to move silently. Getting

caught now would probably just land me in prison, and I still wouldn't have the information I came for.

"The money," I heard her say, "If you'll just take the money and give me my sister back."

He said something I couldn't make out.

"I can't give you that." Her voice sounded agitated. What was he asking for? More money? *Sex?*

I took a risk and slid along the wall, close enough to hear him say. "I don't want any more fucking excuses, Della. I know what you're capable of."

"Not that." She sounded determined now. "I've never done that, and I'm never going to."

Shit, what was he making her do? Should I come out now and just beat the guy to a pulp? From a tactical point of view, it was the stupidest idea I'd ever considered, and yet my hands curled into fists, hungry for his face.

"Caro will be disappointed to hear that," the asshole said. "Especially when I take it out of her flesh."

"Don't you fucking touch her. Where is she? Let me see her."

"Oh, she's a bit... tied up. But I'll tell her you dropped by."

"You're a monster."

He chuckled. "A monster? So dramatic." His hand trailed down her cheek, making me tense. "She likes this monstrous side of me. There was a time you did too."

Her angry gaze shot fire at him. "I never liked a damn thing about you."

"Well, then perhaps you're very good at faking it. Yes,

that must be right."

Now her hands were fists, tucked at her side. "Give me back Caro. Let her go. This is more money than she can possibly give you."

"You think I can't get that much for her? You're probably right, smart girl. As fucked up as she is, and with that pesky drug addiction, she wouldn't be worth more than a thousand. But if I were to rent her out, by the night or by the hour, I'm sure I could make that much."

Della swung at him, and he caught her arm. They exchanged words too quietly for me to hear. From their body language, I understood that Della had not given him everything he wanted—but she was capitulating for now. She turned to leave, her movements jerky. She tried to hide the swipe at her cheek, but I saw the glistening trail. He'd made her cry.

And I was going to make him pay.

It seemed that he was letting her leave, so I waited for her to walk away. Once I was alone with this asshole, we'd have a little one-on-one talk. Yeah, I knew I should talk with Della first. But I couldn't wait for that, not when I was already inside his house, not when I'd seen him put his hands on her.

But when I would have stepped out of the shadows, he turned and walked over to a place in the wall. Frosted glass separated from the slate-tiled wall beside it, and a woman stepped out. I couldn't see much of her—except her blonde hair. *If you'll just take the money, and give me my sister back.* Was this the sister? And she was being held for some sort of ransom?

Not for money, though. What did he want from Del-la?

The man put his arm around the woman's shoulder and led her back inside the room she'd come from. The frosted glass shut again and looked like a decorative panel in the wall. My body tensed. It would be so easy to go after them, to smash the guy's face in and take the girl. Except I had dealt with enough hostage situations over-seas to know how sticky they could get. I didn't even have transportation for her once I got her.

Plus there was no telling if she'd go with me willingly. He was the devil she knew, and I was a stranger.

Captives got weird ideas about their captors some-times.

We studied that shit during training, how to with-stand physical torture and mental manipulation. I could've taken someone whaling on me all day and all night. But watching this girl in trouble, seeing Della scared, feeling helpless in this situation I didn't under-stand yet, that was the true torture.

# CHAPTER NINE
## DELLA

MY HANDS WERE still shaking as I pulled into my neighborhood.

I hated that Dmitri could still affect me this way. I wanted to be tough. No way did Clint start shivering in the middle of some important battle. No way did tears track down his cheeks. *Fuck Dmitri and his ridiculous house.* No, it was a mansion. He had let me wander around for a while. I'm sure it amused him to see me lost and afraid. I had felt him watching from the walls.

And then at the end. Bring the package to me by tonight or you'll receive a package of your own tomorrow morning.

There were a hundred things that could mean, and all of them were horrifying. My sister's body parts, mostly. Or maybe just a picture of her dead body. Or an official visit from some dirty cop on his payroll, offering me fake condolences that they'd found my sister in some ditch.

I turned into my driveway and got out. My neighbor was on her porch, and I almost waved before I realized it wouldn't do any good. But she must have heard my truck, because she stepped onto the lawn and crossed over.

"Hey! Della!"

"Good morning," I said, wincing at her cheery tone. Damn, I wasn't in a good headspace to play the friendly neighbor. Even if Katie was sweet and pretty. *Exactly the kind of girl Clint should end up with.* I should probably introduce them, but I already knew I wouldn't. Because that was the kind of girl I was—in other words, not a very nice one.

"I heard you leave earlier this morning. I was just watering my plants." She gestured back toward her porch, where a huge assortment of potted plants overflowed.

Katie was legally blind, although she could make out shapes sometimes if the lighting was right. She had a great support system of family who came by. Must be a family of lawyers or something, because the guys wore suits, jackets missing, shirts rumpled like they'd had a long day at the office. Sometimes they'd wave hello. One even offered to check my mail while I was away, which I had declined because who knew what crazy shit Dmitri might send me?

"I had some errands to run," I said, clutching my purse tighter. I should have known a deal like that wouldn't work. In fact, I did know, but desperate times and all that.

Even back then, as a small-time dealer, he'd been pretty flush. I had made more money as a stripper on a single night than a full week as a stewardess. Multiply that times all the girls who worked there, and Dmitri had been making a lot of dough. That didn't count the money he made dealing drugs or guns.

An uneasy expression crossed Katie's face. "Actually, I hope you don't mind if I just... I wanted to..."

There was this pause that could have been anything. Maybe Dmitri really *did* send me something horrible and one of his thugs had managed to beat me here. That seemed unlikely though. The thought that really stuck with me was, what if Clint had already met Katie? Maybe he'd ignored my warning to stay inside. I could just imagine him, shirtless, fixing some random broken thing on my house. And Katie wandering over with a glass of lemonade. *Fuck.*

But then Katie did something strange, and all my thoughts evaporated.

When she left home, she had a walking stick that helped her get by, but she didn't use it just outside the lawn. In the bright sunlight, she could see well enough. That was what she'd told me, and it seemed to be true as she stepped right up to the bed of my truck. She leaned over, looking in, her blue eyes not focused on anything.

"Katie?" I asked.

She reached inside. Her hand groped the plastic tarp there, making me wonder where that had come from. It was mine. I had used it to cover the antique sofas and brand-new mattress I'd bought after moving in. I usually kept the tarp in the garage so it wouldn't fly away if the wind kicked up on the highway. But there it was, in Katie's hands as she pulled it up and over, like a magician doing a reveal.

"Do you see anything?" she asked, a hint of anxiety in her voice.

"No... Katie, what's going? Is everything okay?" I took the tarp from her then, because it was clear that something was *not* okay, but holding the dirty old piece of plastic wouldn't help anything.

She let me take the tarp and pointed into the bed of the truck. "You're sure nothing's there. No one is... there. Where did you go, exactly? Did you see someone back here?"

I looked inside at the metal floor of the truck. There were an old pair of boots I used for gardening and a few odds and ends that proved I wasn't very tidy. But certainly not a *person,* which was what her words implied.

"Katie, there's only you and me here." *And Clint in the house.* But I left that part off. The less people who knew about him, the better.

Especially if he suddenly disappeared.

She was reaching over the side of the truck, trying to feel around at the bottom. Her arms didn't quite reach.

"Sweetie?" I asked, uncertain and a little bit scared. What if being alone in that house, with visitors only every other day, had made her a little unhinged? All that solitude sounded like bliss to me, but then I'd been cursed with an overabundance of contact from an early age.

"I thought I saw something," she finally confessed, stepping back on her heels. "I can't make things out too well. There are barely shapes, much less faces. But this morning when I was watering my plants, hidden behind that one azalea with the wild branches, I heard something from your house. I thought it was you, so I almost said hello, but then I noticed how fast it was moving, real low to the ground. And wider than you."

A shiver ran through me. "Lower and wider, huh? Maybe it was an animal. Like a dog or a cat."

"Maybe," Katie said, her voice doubtful. Doubting the idea of an animal or doubting herself? It must be tough to not know what you saw, to be afraid of shadows that would never become clear.

I glanced back into the bed of truck—which was definitely empty. Whatever Katie had or hadn't seen slinking around my truck this morning was gone. The tarp was pretty heavy in my arms, so I rolled it into a rough ball and walked it over to the garage.

When I returned to the truck, I said, "I'm sorry," even though I wasn't sure what for. Because Katie had been worried. Because she'd been wrong. But mostly because I really had to go inside. After the awful meeting with Dmitri this morning and this strange scare, I was ready for a hot bath and a long nap. Preferably with a sexy soldier to keep me company during both of them.

❖    ❖    ❖

MY ANXIETY LEVEL rose when I searched the house and found it empty.

"Clint," I called from the central living room, but only silence answered me.

I'd specifically ordered him to stay put, and he'd defied me, which pissed me off more than anything else. But I was also worried about him. What if Dmitri had sent some guys and picked up "the package" himself? There were no signs of a struggle, and I had to believe a trained soldier could at least put up a fight, even if they had sent three or four guys. And even if they had caught him by surprise.

The other disconcerting thought was that he might have returned to that bitch he'd been with. The one who had ditched him when he'd just come back from a long deployment, right when he'd needed her most. If she'd met him at the airport, he wouldn't have looked twice at me. He wouldn't be at my house right now. *He'd be safe.* Or at least, safer than he was now, disappeared to some mysterious place.

I forced myself to sit on the couch and keep a book open, even though I had no idea what the pages said. Was he okay? What if he'd just run to the store? Should I call the police?

The irony was enough to knock me over.

I did fall, partially, staggering off the cushions and up the stairs. Clint's faded green duffel bag was still sitting in the guest bedroom. His toothbrush was still in the bathroom. *There.* He wouldn't have gone too far without his stuff. *Unless he hadn't gone willingly.*

But I couldn't think like that. I should go downstairs and have a cup of tea. *And wonder what Dmitri was doing to my sister right now.* It was killing me that I hadn't seen her. Hadn't spoken with her since that phone call. We weren't even close, really. Not since we were kids. Things had gotten tense when we were both working at the club, and Dmitri knew how to play our sibling rivalry to the fullest. Next thing I knew, Caro was stepping onto the stage during my dances and giving my regulars a free ride. Anything I said got twisted as if I was the one making trouble for her.

When Dmitri left to make his big deal overseas, I'd been so relieved. *Let's get regular jobs. Regular lives. We still have each other.* Only Caro had been pissed at getting left behind. She had something going with him, which I suspected meant he fucked her whenever he wanted and ignored her the rest of the time. So it wasn't a huge surprise that she'd hooked up with him again as soon as he was back in town.

The surprise had been the "delivery" request, along with the thinly veiled threat to my sister.

I couldn't let her die. Even if she'd gotten herself into this. Even if she should have known better. God, sometimes it killed me that she knew how awful he was but she still went to him. Despite all that, I couldn't let her get hurt.

Clint's bag was sitting against the wall, zipped up and unassuming. I remembered what he'd said that night in bed with me, about the list he had. I'd been out of my mind with lust, teetering on the edge of the sharpest climax of my life, but I'd heard him. It wasn't hard to figure out that Dmitri wanted that list.

What if I gave it to him?

It seemed like a long shot, about as long of a shot as the eight thousand bucks had been. Dmitri would probably shoot me on sight once he found out I knew about the list. And he wasn't the kind of man to leave a loose end alone. And Clint would definitely be a loose end.

*You think he just left something that important lying around?*

I didn't know where he'd leave something like that. If I ever came across something that volatile, that dangerous, I'd run the hell away from it. I didn't seek out trouble, but it had a way of finding me, like burs that stuck to my feet as I walked through the forest. They stung me on contact and left little pricks in my skin even when I pulled them out.

*Are you going to violate Clint's privacy now?*

Clint's privacy was the least of my worries. His life... now that was a big worry.

My decision made, I glanced behind me at the empty hallway and knelt in front of the bag. The zippers weren't locked. No precautions had been taken, which led me to believe Clint was trusting in general. Either that or he just trusted me. Neither idea sat well with me.

Passport.

Dog tags.

Some paperwork from the US Government with cryptic-sounding words.

If I'd had any doubts about his military status, they

were settled now. This man was a soldier, a member of the US Army, a goddamn hero. I should be doing my part to protect him, not drag him into this. *He dragged himself into this.* It would be a relief to believe that, but he hadn't written the orders to send himself overseas and fight some faceless cartel assholes. Assholes like Dmitri's associates.

There were stacks of clothes, plain T-shirts of worn cotton and jeans. The familiar scent of him—musky and comforting—wafted up from the fabric as I pushed it aside. I didn't deserve that comfort. At the bottom of the bag I found a few books, some history books and a well-worn copy of the Bible. That raised my eyebrows.

A religious freak?

They would come by the strip club some nights, passing out pamphlets and telling us we'd go to hell. But Clint hadn't seemed particularly religious. He'd been living with that other girl without being married to her. And he'd taken my confession of being a stripper with more grace than most guys would.

I opened the book, surprised anew at the highlights and underlines and unreadable scribbles in the margin. This Bible wasn't lip service to a childhood commandment. He had read this. He'd studied it.

I opened to a random highlighted line: *for all have sinned and fall short of the glory of God.*

That one was highlighted, and I snorted. Yeah, that was true enough. I had no moral high ground to stand on, but I saw guys in the club who did. Doctors and professors and politicians who'd talk a lot of shit about cleaning up society; meanwhile they'd be sneaking in through the back door to buy drugs and a pair of girls for an hour. We were dirty, all of us. Except Clint, I suspected.

And another: *For I am with you, and no one is going to attack and harm you, because I have many people in this city.*

My smile slipped. Wouldn't that be fabulous? A savior. My own personal GI Joe with an army to back him up. It was too good to be true.

Wasn't it? Clint may be a member of the army, but I wasn't sure he had many people in this city. I wasn't sure he'd be able to protect me from an attack, and he sure as hell wouldn't be able to protect Caro. And if he knew what I'd done, he wouldn't even be with me anymore.

*Therefore confess your sins to each other and pray for each other so that you may be healed.*

Now there was an idea. Confess my sins to Clint and be healed. If only it worked that way. I had deceived him. I'd plotted to kill him. I would still, most likely, lead him to his death. This kind of truth couldn't set me free; it was a prison, one built with the ironclad knowledge that I deserved his scorn.

I slammed the Bible shut and practically threw it against the wall. It thudded and fell to the ground. *Fuck.*

Swallowing hard, I forced myself to glance into the bottom of the bag again. My heart pounded as if I might find snakes or grenades or something else as equally awful as that Bible.

The only thing left was a dark velvet box about the size of my palm. There was no chance he'd keep some computer disk thing in a jewelry box. I was just snooping now. But I thought of that girl Chelsea and imagined him getting down on one knee. Even though it seemed a little big for a ring.

But she didn't deserve a necklace either, or anything at all. I hated the thought of him looking through the jewelry cases, picking something out for her while she'd been here fucking some guy. It made me a hypocrite to be pissed about what she'd done to him, cheating on him and abandoning him and kicking him out of his own apartment, but I couldn't help it.

*You're just snooping now. No good intentions.*

I had no good intentions, only an illicit curiosity for a man I couldn't really have. A man who was fiercely loyal. What would it feel like to be loved by him? I opened the box to find out.

A medal stared back at me. It did more than that. It punched me in the gut and stole my breath. It shone a spotlight on all the horrible, degrading things in my life, including agreeing to help Dmitri kill this man. The one who had earned this.

"It's a Purple Heart."

The words came from the doorway, and I whipped around, almost dropping the box in my panic. I managed to grab hold of it and ease the lid shut. I set the velvet box in his bag gingerly—as if anything would help now—and stood up.

"I'm so sorry." I bit my lip, forcing the tears back. My throat grew tight. "God, I'm sorry."

"Why?" His expression was bemused.

*For conspiring to kill you.* "For looking through your stuff."

He shrugged. "You were probably wondering where I went."

Then I heard the soft rumble of tires and glanced out the window. I had a clear view of the driveway now that I was standing. A dark sedan, an older model, pulled out and drove away. I looked back at Clint. "Who's that?"

*Please don't say Chelsea.*

"My friend James. You might remember him. He was on the plane with me."

*Thank you, Jesus.*

"Oh," I said, way more casually than I felt. "I didn't know you had plans."

"I didn't. Something came up, and I couldn't leave a note. Sorry about that."

"You don't have to apologize to me." *In fact, I really wish you wouldn't.* "But that doesn't give me a right to look through your stuff. I just... Shit, I don't have an excuse."

He smiled slightly. "Don't worry about it. I'm not super secretive anyway. More of an open book. Only problem is it's a pretty boring story."

I glanced back at the open duffel bag, hesitating. "I'd like to hear it anyway, if you don't mind. All of it, your whole story, but also how you got that medal." Fear thumped as if we were going back in time, as if I'd been his girlfriend and gotten a call with bad news. "You were injured? You have to be injured to get that, right?"

"Yeah." He huffed a laugh. "Kind of a morbid requirement, if you ask me. But they don't ask me. They just hand those things out like candy."

I walked up to him, and there wasn't any artifice in me. It felt strange to approach a man without wanting anything from him—not money, not leniency. It felt naked. I just wanted to be near him.

My hands went up around his neck, and his settled on my waist. We flowed into that kiss like water in a cool brook, slipping and sliding and glinting in the sun. There was no better feeling than the touch of his tongue against mine.

I pulled back, missing the heat of his mouth immediately. My gaze met his, and I shook my head slowly. "You can try to make it seem small, but I'm not buying it. They gave you this medal because you're brave and strong. And even if you didn't have it, I'd already know that about you. You're the most noble man I've ever met."

Something flashed in his eyes, hard and almost bitter. "Noble, huh?"

"Yeah. And loyal. And kind." I hesitated. In some ways it felt like spilling my darkest secret. But something compelled me to say it anyway. "I haven't known a lot of kind men."

Clint reached up and curled a lock of hair behind my

ear. Then he stroked a hand down my temple, my cheek. My neck. "That why you're letting me stay?"

"I don't know," I said honestly. I wasn't sure if I kept him here because I liked him or so I could deliver him to Dmitri, which just went to show how fucked up I was. Love or kill. There was no in-between in my world, no gray area. Only absolutes.

I thought he might ask me more questions and demand some answers this time—Lord knew he deserved them. Instead he bent his head and kissed me again, featherlight and painfully sweet. *Ahhh yes.* And when he pulled my body flush against his, I knew exactly what to do. I couldn't give him my loyalty. There would be no medal waiting for him at the end of this. But I could give him my body—my tongue and my pussy and all the roughing up his cute ass could take.

Reaching around behind him, I squeezed the hard cheeks of his ass. He clenched them in response, which made it almost impossible to press my fingers in. Unless I used my nails. He made a sound like a yelp—of surprise, of surrender.

"Jesus," he said against my mouth.

I smiled, not breaking the kiss. I wanted to kiss him with smiles and frowns and everything in between. I would fuse myself to him with glue made of sexual pleasure alone, because that was the only thing I knew how to make.

"You like a little pain, soldier?" I whispered.

He didn't answer, and I thought he wasn't going to.

That was okay. In some ways it was a rhetorical question. I'd already noted his excitement, the throbbing of his cock when I squeezed a little too tight. But when he did respond—Lord, that was sweet.

"I'm not sure." In halting words, he said, "Sometimes when I'm beating one out, I'll squeeze my... my balls. Real tight. I don't even realize I'm doing it until I come."

The mental image of him laid out on a little cot, his body too long and strung up with self-contained lust, was enough to make my body shudder for him. I imagined his eyes shut tight and his fist shut tight and his hand closed tight around his balls, everything coiled and tense and painful until he climaxed in long, ropy sprays.

"What else?" I asked, surprised I could still talk. My voice was husky with a breathlessness born of desire, but I knew he liked me this way. I knew because his eyes widened and his whole body went still. There was a part of me that wanted a repeat of last night, where I pushed and poked and prodded at him until he lost control. Then he would flip me over and fuck me. He'd make me come.

There was a thrill in winding up a man, then letting him stomp around on the ground like a toy monkey with a drum set. It was a cold kind of power.

But a greater part of me wanted to give him orders that he'd follow. To hurt him and please him and control him in a way that wasn't cold. It was so damn hot I might incinerate just from thinking about it.

"I pinch my nipples sometimes," he said, and I almost

came on the spot. It took two deep breaths to get myself under control.

Then I said, "Show me." All calm and collected, as if I watched men strip for me every day. I was the one who stripped, who bared myself. With every other man, in every other way. But Clint took off his shirt and tossed it on the ground. He gave me a nervous look, as if I might stop him now. *As if.* Then he looked down at his chest and pressed a nipple between his thumb and forefinger.

"Is that how you usually do it?" I asked. "That soft?"

"No, I—" His cheeks colored a deep shade of plum. Like the head of his cock must be. "Harder."

I pinched his other nipple. "Like this?"

He made a strangled sound. *"Della."*

It wasn't technically an answer, but I let it slide. Or maybe I didn't, because when I twisted his nipple, it felt a little like punishment. Especially when he sucked in a sharp breath and closed his eyes. That was fine with me, though. I could look at the length of him, from the broad shoulders to the tapered hips to the thighs so lovingly encased by old denim.

Oh, and his cock. The erection had grown to impressive proportions beneath his fly. He'd have to be careful with that zipper on its way down.

"Take off your pants. And your underwear, if you're wearing any."

The look he gave me was filled with desperation. For me to go easier? Or harder? It didn't really matter. I'd never had this much control over a man this strong. It was heady, intoxicating. Was this how people felt when they shot chemicals into their veins? I'd tried it a couple times and only felt dizzy and sick. This, though. This was a miracle.

He stripped and waited for instructions. What a good boy. What a *big* boy.

I knelt in front of him, ignoring his murmured, half-hearted protests. *You don't have to. Let me...* But this wasn't for him, not really. I wanted to taste his cock, so I did. *Salty. Earthy.* I wanted to watch him squirm, so I licked the crown of his cock and the slit on the top until he was panting and humping my mouth. It should have been degrading for him, humiliating the way those paid sex acts had always been for me, but he just looked so beautiful. He looked like an angel with his body rippling and shaking, and I couldn't help but admire him.

"I can't stop," he said in a half shout.

I wondered idly if Katie could hear him. Part of being a good neighbor was not making a lot of noise, so I pulled back. I undressed slowly, loving his gaze on me and the little moans he made as the air whispered over his damp cock. My panties came off last, and I folded them so that the little wet spot I'd left would fit right on his tongue.

"Bite down," I said, and he did, with a little sucking noise that told me he tasted my arousal. He drank it down. "And keep your teeth together. If those panties fall out before we're done, you're going to be in trouble."

His hips rocked forward. He nodded his agreement, gaze unfocused and glazed with arousal. Most of the fabric hung over his chin, only the dampest part in his mouth, held there by his teeth. It was another thing that could have seemed silly, pink lace hanging from his lips. On him it just looked obscene, as if he'd torn it off some unsuspecting girl's ass. As if he were a wild animal, a wild *sex* animal who ripped undergarments on a rampage.

I found a condom in the side table and rolled it on him. "Put your hands behind your back." He did as instructed and scooted into the V of my legs when I perched on the bed. "Now fuck me. Good and hard. Fuck me until I come, but don't let go of those panties. And you don't get to come until I do."

It took him a little while to get his cock lined up. He didn't have his hands to help guide him in or position my hips. And I certainly wasn't going to help. The height didn't *quite* match up, but that only made it sweeter. I could sit there with my legs spread, half reclined on the bed. Meanwhile he had to bend his legs in an awkward angle and nudge at my swollen pussy lips.

Even once he was lined up, I knew he was holding back, afraid to slam into me, afraid to get the angle wrong and hurt me instead. I suppose I could have reached down and helped, but I did something else instead. I pinched his nipple. And then when he made a little groaning sound—a sound that had my pussy clenching around the tip of his cock—I pinched him even harder. I even used my nails a little, grinding them into his skin until he had no choice at all, until his hips bucked and he was fully impaled inside me.

It took him by surprise, ending up inside me. It must have felt good, because the muscles in his neck corded and his eyes rolled back. He almost dropped the panties then, but he managed to catch them—by the curl of his tongue, I thought. He sucked in a breath and practically chewed on the fabric as he struggled to hold on.

Watching him fight and clench and wriggle in sensual torture was the hottest thing I'd ever seen. I felt electrified, current running all over my skin in a sexual barbed wire I couldn't get out of. So I did the only thing left to me: I reached my fingers down and circled my clit. I played with myself until my pussy released hot liquid, bathing his cock. Even through the condom, he felt that, his body tensing. The muscles in his arms were particularly bulging. He must have been working hard to keep his hands behind his back.

I slapped the side of his ass. "Move, soldier."

A furious sound emerged as he pulled away and pushed back in. He was so fucking close to coming. The plum color suffused his cheeks again—and yes, it did match the head of his cock. It was hurting him to hold back, but this was one pain I wouldn't regret giving him.

I eased up on my clit so I could last longer. I made him fuck me for fifteen more minutes, sometimes changing the angle so that I backed away from my orgasm. All the while, I pinched and flicked and licked his chest, drawing him ever closer to climax. The sounds he made grew frantic and tortured. He begged me with incoherent sounds, muffled by my panties, his message clear. *I need to come. Please let me come.* On one particularly vicious stroke of my nails down his chest, the choked sound was mournful. *I'm already coming. I'm sorry I disobeyed you. Forgive me.*

When he could open his eyes, I gave him my sternest look. "You couldn't even help yourself, could you? Just rutted like a dog until you came, not thinking about me at all."

I could have sworn his cock twitched inside me, even softening as it was. He loved this shit, and God help me, so did I.

He turned and opened his mouth, letting the panties fall to the floor. His voice was raw. "I couldn't hold back."

"On your knees, then. I'll just have to teach you how to please a woman. And not with that selfish cock of yours."

When he knelt by the bed, it reminded me of prayer. But he wasn't asking favors of a disinterested God, wasn't reading his tattered Bible right now. I pressed his face into my pussy and made him lick up the mess he had made. I came three times that way, imagining his tongue forming ancient words of communion and demise. *Confess your sins,* he would say, and I rode his face to a blinding orgasm. *Pray for each other,* he would say, and I yanked his hair until he groaned, sending vibrations through my clit.

By the time my legs cramped from staying open that long, he was hard again. I bent him over the side of the bed and started playing all over again.

# CHAPTER TEN
## CLINT

I WATCHED HER sleep, her eyelids moving as she dreamed her way through an afternoon nap.

Pretty sure I was the creepy guy in this scenario, sitting on a chair in the corner, elbows on my knees, watching her. Like when I'd followed her in the truck. I was becoming a full-fledged psycho, and I had to wonder if it was related to my recent mission. I'd heard of it happening to guys. They passed the psych evals, then went home and dragged their wife behind a couch to take cover from an imaginary grenade.

Not me, though. You never think that will be you. But as I sat there, I couldn't have told you if I was going through some kind of stress hallucination. Was there really a threat to Della? Or did my mind make that up because that was how it viewed the world now—through violence, through fear?

I stood and kissed her cheek before settling the blanket tighter around her. She sighed softly and curled her hands into fists beneath her chin, childlike.

Della and I had fucked for hours, literally. The last time she'd come, shaking and shuddering beneath me, she'd drifted off to sleep almost immediately. I'd still had my dick inside her, hard, primed to come, but I'd pulled out. Didn't want to disturb her. I hoped she slept for a long time, deep and restorative. *The sleep of the dead.* That was what my foster mother used to call it.

If another guy had told me he was worried about going off the deep end, I'd have told him to call the counselors at the VA. *Make an appointment. Don't do anything rash. Keep a cool head.* You know those things are the safe thing to do, the smart thing. But I was too wired to fight, too certain this was true.

Something bad was going to happen, and it would happen soon.

I heard the distant buzz of my cell phone from the guest room. I left Della to sleep, shutting the door behind me. James's grinning face flashed on my screen.

"What did you find?"

James was all business, which told me it was bad. "Had to trace it through a bunch of shell corporations. Fucking money trail. They put up a lot of roadblocks just to find out who owned that land."

"Pretty suspicious."

"Yeah, especially when one connection kept showing up. Dmitri Ozerov."

"Fuckin' A."

I could almost hear James's nod over the line. He'd been my contact when I was undercover. I was in the field, puffed up and acting like some kind of badass. Didn't have access to my laptop or anything. That was what James was for. I'd feed him information, which he'd pass on to the higher-ups. He'd also clue me in about the people and their businesses so I'd be able to work them better.

We both recognized the name Dmitri Ozerov. Not a major player compared to the guys we took down, but when you were talking about international terrorism affiliations, everyone was trouble.

"That must've been who I saw," I said. "Didn't get a close look at him, but I wouldn't have recognized him anyway. We got a recent photograph?"

"I'm sending you one now, along with a domestic rap sheet. Lots of shit going on here. Drugs. Guns. Flesh trade." There was a weighted pause. "How'd your girl get mixed up in all this?"

*She's not my girl.* I wasn't sure that was true. She felt like mine, even if I shouldn't get involved that fast. Shouldn't fall that fast. I'd always fallen fast, and that was before I met Della. She was too damned perfect, like my wet dreams and deepest hopes come to life.

"I don't know," I admitted to James—and admitted to myself that I didn't know her at all. Just saw her sexy little swagger and the mixture of wonder and fear in her eyes. She was a contradiction, and I wanted her, all of her, no part left undesired.

"What's next?" James asked. It was something he'd said to me on those untraceable phone calls while I was undercover.

"Find out the connection."

Another pause. "Snoop around on Della. Don't you think that's…"

Creepy? Yeah. "Just do it. I think this whole thing is going to come down on our heads."

"Wait, you don't mean the list, right?"

I shrugged, suspicion a tight knot in my chest. *She doesn't owe you loyalty.* No, but I wanted her to. "I just think it's a little fucking suspicious that my life consists of Pop-Tarts and late-night television for twenty-one years. Then suddenly I'm in possession of a criminal list and I happen to meet a beautiful girl with ties to some arms dealer."

"I don't know, man. People run into trouble all the time. Doesn't have to be related."

"No, but I want you to find out how she knows him. How often she sees him." *Whether she's fucking him.* But that would be implied. If there was any information like that available, James would pass it on. He always had before.

"You ever heard of imposter syndrome?" James said with his usual attitude. "Means you don't think you're good enough to deserve something. So maybe you fuck it up on purpose because then you're back in your comfort zone."

"Thank you, Dr. Phil. Are you finished?"

"Not really, because I'm saying if she gets wind that you had her investigated—"

"This isn't an imposter-syndrome thing. It's not a PTSD thing." *I'm not fucking crazy.* "There's a threat here. I saw him with her, okay? She wasn't happy to see him."

"All right. Okay. If you say that's how it is…"

"I'm saying so," I said firmly. "Anyway, you've seen Della. It's not stupid to question why she's with me. She's a ten and a half. Would you really think I deserve her?"

"Hell fucking yes," James said, as serious as I'd ever heard him. "If anyone deserves to find a nice, beautiful girl to fuck all night, it's you."

*Shit.* My chest panged with some feeling I didn't recognize. My throat tightened, and I had to end the conversation. "Find out the connection, okay? I need to know what I'm working with."

*So maybe you fuck it up on purpose because then you're back in your comfort zone.*

After hanging up, I went to my open duffel bag and picked up the hard case inside. Flipped it open. Stared at the purple ribbon and glinting gold and wondered if it would ever mean something good to me. All I remembered was blood and fear and the certainty that I was going to die. Shrapnel had gone deep into my arm, splicing the nerves and spilling dark liquid down the front of my gear. Smoke and dust and sweat turned the air into a solid material, one I struggled to breathe. William and I weren't friends. I had barely recognized him as another operative with the shaggy hair and long-ass blonde beard. He'd looked otherworldly like that, pale eyes, pale skin. He'd fit right in.

At the end, when we'd gathered enough evidence to

convict and the military force arrived to shut them down, I was supposed to get out. It was too dangerous to stick around, in case the terrorists made me for a spy. But then someone had suspected William, which was of course a valid concern. They tortured him a little. Some burns. Bashed his knee in. Kicked him around until he stopped opening his eyes. My choice was to take him with me or leave him to die.

So I'd taken him with me and disobeyed a direct order to do it. Didn't that beat all? Disobeyed an order and got a fucking medal. I couldn't get over that.

It made me feel like I'd been doing the right thing when I kept that data to myself. It had come from William, with a whispered warning about two days before he'd gotten himself tortured. *Don't trust anyone with this.* Turned out to be good advice. He still hadn't come out of his coma, last I heard.

I hadn't trusted anyone since then either, except James. And Della. I didn't want to be making a mistake with her. Whatever we had going—the sex, the chatting over coffee in our pjs, the fixing up her house—I wanted it to be real.

BEFORE HEADING OUTSIDE, I tucked my pistol into the waistband of my jeans and tried not to think about what that meant. I just didn't know what I was dealing with, whether this guy Dmitri would come over drunk and waving a gun around like some deranged ex-lover. Or maybe the next time Della went to see him, he wouldn't let her leave. The point was, until I knew what I was dealing with, I wanted to be prepared.

So when I stepped onto the porch and heard rustling in the garage, my skin prickled in warning. I lifted my chin, like an animal scenting danger. I didn't smell the chemical tang of explosives or the gasoline of Humvees, though. There was just honeysuckle and a crisp summer scent.

Silently I moved off the porch and through the grass. The back of the garage provided more cover, so I circled around. A quick scan of the street told me no new vehicles had arrived. Whoever this was had come on foot.

I paused, listening. There was nothing for a moment, then a quiet shuffle of something being moved and set down carefully. It destroyed the possibility of a raccoon rummaging through her trash bins, which I already knew were stored inside.

After a beat I pushed inside and pointed my gun at the intruder. "Hands where I can see them."

The person jumped in surprise, then slowly lifted her arms above her head. She was standing near the trash bins—not near my boxes. *Not looking for the list.* She had dark blonde hair and a small stature, but I didn't let my guard down. Danger came in all shapes and sizes, including attractive women. *Including attractive women like Della.*

"Turn around," I said.

The woman turned slowly, her expression calculating.

Her eyes were a deep blue—and focused on me like a hawk's. "Oh, it's you."

I raised my eyebrows. "We met before?"

"No, but I've seen you around." She smiled, but it didn't seem friendly. More like she'd thought of a joke only she knew. "I live next door. Your friend knows me as Katie."

I flicked my gaze behind her. "There a reason you're going through her trash?"

"Just doing my job." She didn't lower her hands but pushed her right hip out. "Shield's in here if you want to see it."

*Fuck.* Her shield? Then she was some kind of LEO—shorthand for law enforcement officer. Police? FBI? It didn't fucking matter, because if a LEO was on the scene, things were about to get a whole lot stickier. It could have been a trap to pull me closer and let my guard down, but she was too matter-of-fact. And the way she spoke to me, it was as if she knew about my training. I suspected she had a guy who ran background checks and gathered intel for her the same way James did for me. After months of being undercover, I could recognize that in someone else.

All the same, I said, "Turn around. Hands on the wall."

I kept the gun pointed at her until I pulled the identification out of her pocket and read it. Then I lowered my gun and held out the badge. "Good to meet you, Agent Katherine Porter."

Her lids lowered, telling me she'd caught the sarcasm

in my words. Good. At least whoever they'd sent to mess with Della wasn't an idiot. "Good to meet you too, Specialist Clint Adams. Now you want to tell me what you're doing here? And don't tell me you're doing your job. I've already checked. There are no other agencies supposed to be here."

"I'm not a fucking agency. I'm a random guy bumming a place to stay."

"Random, huh?"

Yeah, I had to admit that was seeming less likely as time ticked by. "What do you got against Della?" I asked, not really expecting her to tell me.

"Nothing. We know she cut ties to Dmitri, or at least tried to."

"Oh good. I guess you'll be on your way."

Agent Porter made a sour face. "Her sister, however…"

Her sister was being held for ransom, as best I could tell from the conversation I'd overheard. That was some bad shit. The FBI could definitely help. Or they'd make it worse. One or the fucking other.

"If Dmitri Ozerov is your target, then why don't you go arrest him?"

"You of all people know it's never that simple."

Oh yeah. Gather evidence. Sit back while innocent people get raped and killed. Tell yourself it would pay off in the end even though William was still in the hospital and the people they arrested would probably plea bargain out. Being the good guy was a regular old good time.

"I still don't know what you expect to find in Della's garbage bag." Besides my used condoms. Goddamn FBI. They were worse than a nosy old lady.

She shrugged, a polite way of saying *mind your own business.* "Has Ozerov contacted her while you've been here?"

I ignored her question—for now—and scrubbed a hand over my face. "Un-freaking-believable."

Though I had to admit, the one good thing about this was I knew I wasn't crazy.

"I'll show you mine if you show me yours," Agent Porter said matter-of-factly.

Damn it, I didn't want to agree, but I needed information. Might as well go along with it. And I really had nothing to lose here. *Except Della.* "Fine," I said. "She went to visit him."

"I knew it! Goddamn it. They lost her tail."

I gave her a look that told her exactly how impressed I was with the FBI right now. "I can give you the coordinates and some background info I found about the owners, tracing back to Ozerov. That gonna be enough?"

"Unfortunately no." She took a deep breath. "I'd get in trouble for disclosing this, but I'm going to hold up my end of the bargain. The truth is, we can probably bust Dmitri right now if we wanted to. Nothing major but it would be enough to put him behind bars for five years, and my supervisors would take that much to get him off the streets."

"But?" I prompted.

"But they need a bigger fish. Ozerov thinks he's hot shit but the truth is he's always been small time. Never made much of a mark on the global stage until recently. Something changed. We think he got an accomplice."

"It's not Della," I said flatly. No goddamn way.

"We don't think that," she said quickly. "But we need to find out who it is, and she's our best in."

"She's not your *in*," I said, all my bitterness pouring out of me. Della's secrets. This woman's cool deception. "You're not going to use her for this."

From a distance, I heard the screen door slam. I stiffened, and so did Agent Porter. I managed to tuck my gun in the back of my jeans. A few seconds later, Della rounded the corner looking drowsy and gorgeous.

Confusion flickered on her face before she smiled. "Hey, guys. I see you two met."

"Yeah, uh, I was just out here and—"

Agent Porter cut me off. "It's my fault. I must not have been counting my steps right, because I was standing here trying to get into your garage and he came to see if I was okay."

I glanced at her curiously and saw her eyes staring off into space. Aw fuck, that was low. Pretending to be blind? Very low. She had the sympathy angle. Plus Della wouldn't even know she was being spied on.

Della was gracious about the supposed mistake and even offered to help escort "Katie" back to her porch. I managed not to roll my eyes until they were out of sight. The whole incident had been hugely illuminating, not only because of what Agent Porter had divulged.

Also because I could see Della as the sweet, easy mark that she was.

She had a lot of world-wise vibes she put out, warning people away, almost threatening with that smile sharp as a knife. But she was too trusting to really play the game—and with a sinking feeling, I realized I was too. We wanted to think the best of everyone instead of assuming they'd fuck us over if they could. Della had made that mistake with her neighbor. And I had made that mistake with the pretty stewardess who offered me a ride home.

# CHAPTER ELEVEN
## DELLA

I T WAS ALMOST a relief seeing Clint's face dark and untrusting. Even the hint of hurt I saw in his eyes, as if I'd wounded him, felt right. Like a punch to my gut—losing my breath and knowing I deserved it.

Now he'd demand answers, and I felt almost at peace. He'd know. He'd hate me, but he was already figuring it out without my help. He was putting the puzzle together, when I hadn't even known he had any pieces.

After helping Katie into her house, I returned to mine. Walked right past him despite the soft clatter of dishes in the kitchen. I sat down on my couch, the one I'd been so excited to find at a resale shop with plush rose-gold cushions and maple-wood inlays, and felt out of place in my own house. Felt out of place in Dmitri's gleaming mansion too. I travelled the whole world feeling out of place, because where I really belonged was back in the seedy strip club downtown. Or huddling in the room I shared with Caro while my sister got shot in the living room.

Stealing from her boss, they said. Me and Caro would go work for them, make things right.

Little girls in a strip club. *That* wasn't right.

When Clint came back inside, he was holding something. My cream-colored teacup and matching plate with its gold trim. Steam rose from the top of the cup. He set it down in front of me, and I stared at it. Just stared. It looked like a puzzle. My teacup, my tea. Put right in front of me.

"No one's ever made me tea before," I said, my voice hoarse.

He looked at me strangely—torn. Torn between anger and pity. My stomach turned over. I felt sick, and I took a sip of the tea he'd made to calm myself. Stronger than I usually made it, and had he added honey? So strange to think of someone else's hands preparing a drink for me, to comfort me.

He let me drink half the cup before he spoke.

"I know about Ozerov," he said, and my hand started to shake so badly that the cup rattled against the saucer. I set it down on the table, pushed it away.

"How'd you find out?" I asked. That seemed like the easiest question. Better than *how soon are you going to leave and never come back?* Or *are you going to call the police?* I had to convince him not to. Dmitri would lose his shit if the police came sniffing around. I'd seen him dump ten thousand dollars' worth of drugs in the river when he got questioned once. Another time, the police had dragged him down to the station for questioning. The girl in the makeup vanity next to me disappeared the next day. Didn't matter if she'd really ratted him out.

Didn't matter if my sister had really stolen from him. Another girl ended up dead, and nobody cared. *But I care.* And I wouldn't let that happen to Caro.

"Followed you," Clint said. "Hopped in the back of your truck when you went upstairs and followed you into that place."

*Holy shit.* My first thought was that he was pretty damned stealthy. That must come in handy for his military stuff. My second thought was to wonder why he'd cared enough to see. Was he just bored? Or one of those controlling type of guys who thought I was going to cheat when I tried to buy tampons from the corner store?

"Must have been exciting," I said in a dull voice.

His gaze sharpened. "Exciting? No. The ball game would have been exciting. That was something else." He shook his head. "I can't believe you went there like that. Talk about a fucking lion's den."

I jerked back, stung. "You don't know the situation. And you don't know me."

"So tell me. That's what we're gonna do now. A little getting-to-know-you session."

I hated the hint of mocking in his words. I'd done this. Turned him from a sweet, caring guy into this one, who cursed and intimidated me. He looked about two seconds from walking out that door, and I almost didn't care. Except that my heart would break.

*Except that you still need to do what Dmitri told you to.*

Sometimes you had to make a choice. My sister's life or Clint's. For once I didn't know which one I'd pick, but

I opened my mouth and told him everything. Even if he'd die, at least he'd die knowing. It was the least I could do.

"Dmitri owned the strip club where I worked. Where I was—" I choked on the words a little. I'd barely admitted it to myself, much less to another person. "Where I was forced to work. First in the back rooms. Then when I looked old enough, I moved to the front."

"How old?" he asked sharply.

"Sixteen when I started dancing. With makeup and stilettos you can't hardly tell the difference."

"And the back rooms?"

I pressed my lips together, unable to say much. Not because I didn't want to cooperate or because he didn't deserve the whole truth. Just because I was held together by a thread here, and his derision would feel razor sharp.

"Ten," I said, looking away. "I was ten when I first went to stay there."

"Jesus, Della."

"And the plants died. That's what I thought about at the beginning. I had three plants, and all of them must have died without anyone to water them. I had worried over having to pick one to live and one to die, but in the end, they all died."

He stared at me like he had no fucking clue what I was talking about, but that was all right. None of this really mattered. This wasn't why I'd followed him off the plane.

"Grew up," I said, forcing myself to continue. "Got my GED by mail. Left Dmitri. I told him I was never coming back to him. I thought he might put up a fight, but he didn't really."

"You and Dmitri, were you ever..." He didn't finish. The distasteful expression on his face told me what he thought of the idea.

*I feel the same way.*

"For a little while. First he was with Caro. She's older than me. She filled out faster. Then, I don't know. I guess he got bored or just wanted to start trouble. He came to me and..." I laughed, the sound hollow. My insides were all hollow. Numbness had spread from the inside out, leaving only a shell, the story of my life like the faint ocean sounds you hear inside. "He said I was saving her."

"What the hell's that mean?"

That was one choice in my life that had been easy. Her or me. "I knew he hit her sometimes. Hurt her. He said if I let him touch me, he'd leave her alone. I thought it would make her life easier."

Clint's eyes narrowed, and in the slits, I saw fires burning. Rage directed at Dmitri, and those flames were enough to warm me. Even if I'd probably get consumed by them in the end.

"But she didn't see it that way. She thought I wanted Dmitri to pay attention to me because he'd give me money and jewelry. I didn't *want* his money." It suddenly seemed important that Clint understand that. That he believe me about this. "I never wanted him."

"Okay," he said softly.

All the indignation drained out of me, about as quickly as it had come. "All I've ever wanted is to get away from him. Caro too."

"But you left without her," he said, almost proudly, like he was happy I'd gotten myself out at any cost. *Even sacrificing my sister.* I didn't want to make that choice a second time.

"I couldn't make her go. I thought it would be okay, maybe. Since he let me leave. Figured he might hit her one too many times and she'd get fed up and leave too. I even got this house as soon as I could afford to, so there'd be room enough for both of us."

"She never came." He stated it as a fact.

"No. Not even when Dmitri left town to do his business shit. She found some other guy to live with. Other parties and drugs and whatever else. I don't even know. I barely saw her anymore. I tried to tell myself she was happy that way."

"And now Dmitri is back." Another fact.

"He called me up. I didn't even know he was living here again or that Caro had hooked up with him." I shook my head, embarrassed to admit I hadn't talked to Caro. Hadn't wanted to hear her coked out or drunk off her ass.

Clint's gaze locked on mine. "What did Dmitri ask you to do?"

*Fucking tell him the truth.* He deserved to know. "He wants me to get him something. Some...drugs. Like a shipment thing at the airport."

Sometimes you had to make a choice, and you picked

the cowardly one.

"Why didn't you want to?" Clint asked.

"Because it's illegal. And it's wrong. Really, really wrong, okay?"

"So you offered to give him eight thousand dollars instead?"

I made a face at Clint just so he'd know I wasn't thrilled about the whole hiding-in-my-truck thing. So that was who Katie had seen. But I couldn't exactly claim any moral high ground here, so I moved on. "He didn't take it. It was a long shot, but...I don't know what else to do."

In all honesty, I was hoping Clint would have some kind of magic solution. That was a long shot too, like the eight thousand dollars.

"Have you tried talking to the police?" he asked, and that was when I knew that no magic solution would be happening. The police was dead last on my list of things to try. I'd be dead before I got that far down the list. *Caro would be dead.*

"No, and I'd appreciate it if you wouldn't tell them," I said stiffly. "Dmitri won't react well to that, and he has my sister. He'll kill her."

A little groove appeared between Clint's eyebrows, and I knew he was thinking hard about how to say what he wanted to say. He leaned forward. "I don't deny that he's a dangerous person, but you said your sister was with him for a while. He hurt her, but he didn't kill her then. What makes you think he's going to do it now?"

I stood up and found my phone in my purse. Pulled up the first text message and set the phone on the coffee table in front of him. On the screen was a picture of my sister, eyes swollen. Her skin wasn't skin colored anymore. It was black and blue and purple and red. She barely even looked human.

He picked it up and swore softly. "He did this?"

I shrugged. "Who else? Dmitri has never had a problem getting his hands dirty."

Clint's gaze sharpened. "He did that to you?"

"Not like that. Not on my face. He knew our bodies would heal and you would barely be able to tell anything had ever happened. But faces, they never heal right with something like that. He wouldn't have beaten me like that and lost whatever money I could make on the pole."

"Fuck." He stared at the photograph. "This is unbelievable."

"I figured you would have seen worse things where you went. War zones and all that."

"Not much worse than a woman's face bashed in. But yeah, I've seen some bad shit, but I thought it was mostly over there. We have domestic abuse and crimes in the US, I know that. But what you're talking... that's slavery. That's human trafficking. That is the kind of shit that happens over there every fucking day. And here too, I guess."

"Assholes everywhere," I said, like I was some kind of criminal-world Buddha.

He quirked his lips. "Yeah. Assholes everywhere."

"I don't know if he'll really kill her," I said honestly. "But I know that if he doesn't, it's not out of kindness. He's not that kind. It's just because he wants to keep her around, or maybe he's too cheap to pay off the cops again. I don't know, but I can't take the chance."

Clint nodded slowly, his expression thoughtful. "So what's your plan? You gonna give him what he wants?"

*Maybe. Are you willing to die for me?* "I don't know yet. Just stalling, I guess."

Sometimes you had to make a choice, but I would put this one off for as long as I could.

✧ ✧ ✧

WE MADE IT through the rest of the afternoon as if nothing horrible had happened. Clint even flirted with me with a tenderness I was shocked to see. He kissed me on the tip of my nose, and tears welled in my eyes. I looked away so he wouldn't see them. How could he even look at me after what he knew?

*Because you didn't tell him the whole truth, coward.*

Yeah, but I'd told him a lot of bad shit in my past and he hadn't run screaming. Wouldn't have blamed him if he had, but he didn't. Went out for drinks with his friend James, but left his stuff here. He was coming back, he assured me. He also asked to make sure I'd be okay.

"Stay inside the house," he said. "Don't go any-where."

*Don't go back to Dmitri's house,* he meant.

"I'll stay here," I promised, pretending like everything

was fine even though it wasn't. A current of expectation ran through the air. By tonight, Dmitri had said. I had to deliver him by tonight. Which meant I would have to decide soon.

The rap on the door made me jump. I peered out the kitchen window in time to see a van head down the street. It didn't have its lights on, but I could make out the shape of it—large, looming—and wondered if this was how Katie felt.

As the van passed, a car parked on the street pulled away from the curb and followed. The car had its lights off too. *Strange.* Strange enough to make this feel dreamlike, unreal. I imagined all the cars on the roads with their lights off, gliding through the pitch-black night like fish in the sea. No lights flashing or blinking. Peaceful.

I opened the front door to see, half expecting a pipe bomb to go off in my face. As long as Clint wasn't here to get caught in the blast, I didn't even care.

Instead there was a box.

Not a velvet box like Clint's had been. This one was a similar size but wrapped in brown paper. I knew better than to expect anything good inside, but I felt curiously numb as I carried it to my dining room. The thick brown paper tore to reveal a brown cardboard box, like the kind used for moving, but tiny. I opened it and stared inside.

Horror planted itself in my gut and grew a thick base all the way up to my throat. It branched into cold tendrils that wrapped around my arms and held me in place. It rooted me to the spot, and all I could do was stare inside at the ten fingernails, painted purple. Glittery purple the way Caro had done sometimes.

Oh God. *Caro.*

I didn't know how much time had passed. I thought I might have blacked out for a few minutes. Or a few hours. When I came to again, my mouth tasted of vomit.

They weren't even that bloody. That was what I thought about. There was some blood, on the ones that had flipped over. And some black stuff that I thought might be flesh. But not puddles of blood like I would have thought.

Calmly, my hands steady, I closed the box and threw it in the trash. Then I took the trash out to the big trash container in the garage. Then I went back inside my house and threw up again.

I heard gravel crunch as a car pulled into the driveway. Another van? *Another package?*

Then the door slammed and I heard Clint's voice call my name. Relief filled me, because he'd come back. He'd come back, and now I could save my sister.

# Chapter Twelve

## Clint

JAMES AND I actually went to a bar, the way I told Della we would. But instead of drinking beer and playing darts, we went over the intel James had gathered. The information about Dmitri might help me protect Della. Or I could use it as leverage with the FBI agent. I'd have to play it by ear.

Everything he'd found backed up what Della had told me. Which was good, except that I got the feeling she was hiding something from me. Something important.

"What's next?" James said as we left the bar and headed back toward Della's place.

"That depends. You up for a little field trip?"

"Christ, yes. Get me out of the van." There wasn't an actual van, but since vans were so often used for surveillance, James used the phrase. He was great at providing support, but I knew sometimes he wanted to stretch his legs.

"Not tonight. Tomorrow. I want to find out if the sister is at the same location or if he's keeping her somewhere else. The picture of her..." I shook my head. "He messed her up pretty bad."

James's gaze sharpened. "You think she's still alive."

"Hard to say. Some proof of life would be nice."

"If your girl starts asking for that, odds are Dmitri will get suspicious. He'll think she's called in the FBI."

"She may not have called them, but they are here." I glanced at the neighboring house. The windows were dark, but I had no doubt a telescope pointed from one of those windows. Someone was watching. "Anyway, I don't really want to suggest that to her. She's freaked out enough as it is without thinking her sister may already be dead."

I glanced back at James, whose expression was smug.

"You like her," he said.

"No shit, Sherlock."

"You *really* like her."

"Yeah, and we're sitting in a tree, K-I-S-S-I-N-G. Can we be done with this bullshit and focus?"

James sobered. "You had to fall for a girl with major underworld connections, didn't you? I'm just saying, push comes to shove, you can't be sure which way she'll go."

Actually, I was pretty damn sure she would choose her sister over me. I couldn't even blame her. James had dug up some background information. A father serving a life sentence, no hope for parole. Mother gone. Her oldest sibling had been murdered, her body found off the pier with a bullet in her brain. The middle sister was the only family Della had left. If I'd had any family, I would have guarded them with my life too.

"I always fall for girls," I said, trying to make light of

it. "Doesn't mean it's a real thing."

"You always fall for girls," James said skeptically.

"You have specifically mocked me for doing so, so yeah, I'd say that's true. I always fall for girls, too fast and too hard. Then they end up leaving, and you mock me."

"Thank you for that rousing portrait of me as a friend. What I'm saying is that you're into the girls. You say nice things about them. You *think* nice things about them. You will give them a key to your whole life if they blink at you. But you don't fall for them. Not really."

"What's the difference, then? How is Della different?" I was bullshitting, though, because Della *was* different. I just didn't know why. Beautiful, yes. Classy, yes. The greatest lay I'd ever had, yes. But there were other women. What made this one like honey, so sweet I couldn't get enough?

James shrugged. "How many times did you e-mail Chelsea while you were overseas, huh?"

"I was undercover. Kind of hard to send her cat gifs and corny lines."

"You didn't e-mail her. You didn't call her. You barely mentioned her. Bet you didn't even jack off to thoughts of her."

"Come on."

"Come on, what? You'll give them money, your apartment. You'll give them anything they want, except yourself. You're a fucking bleeding heart, but you don't let girls in."

I stayed silent.

His tone softened. "Compare that to now, where we're out having some secret vigilante meeting just for this girl. And you can't stop talking about her. It's Della this and Della that. You practically broke my arm when you realized how late it was. *Have to check on her.*"

"This is what I'm talking about. The mocking."

"The mocking is just because I'm an asshole. But this girl is doing something to you. It's like black fucking magic, and I'm not gonna lie, it makes me nervous."

❖   ❖   ❖

SOMETHING HAD CHANGED in the hour I'd been gone. The house felt different—the air sharper, the lights more eerie.

"Della!" I called, my heart pounding. She would be okay. She had to be okay.

"I'm up here," she said, and I released a breath of pure relief.

"I'll just shower," I said from outside her door. "I smell like smoke now."

Maybe it was presumptuous to assume she'd even care what I smelled like. Just because we'd had sex the past two nights didn't mean we'd have it again tonight. And she might be feeling raw from having told me all that personal stuff. I wasn't going to push that part, but I did want to sleep with her. Like actually lie in the same bed with my arm around her waist and hold her all night.

After stepping out of the shower, I toweled off and pulled on a loose pair of sweatpants. Her door was still closed, and I wanted to check on her. Hell, I wouldn't push the sleeping together thing either, but I had to know she was okay.

I knocked on her bedroom door, lightly. When she didn't answer, I called, "Della?"

More knocking went unanswered. More calls went unacknowledged. *Shit.* What if she was sleeping? Or what if she was in trouble? I couldn't just leave her without checking.

These were the moments I wondered if I was being too aggressive with her. Wondered whether I'd even know the line between aggressive and protective anymore. I imagined some courtroom, dissecting the mental breakdown of a special ops soldier. Exhibit A, paranoid delusions. Exhibit B, ignored social cues, like the fact that failure to respond to knocking usually indicates lack of interest.

Exhibit C, called "I'm coming in," and stepped inside the room, uninvited.

Exhibit D, stopped and stared at the beautiful woman wearing a black and red lace bra and matching panties. Black garter belts covered her legs for miles. And those heels. Oh Jesus fuck, those heels. I'd dream of them walking on me for the next ten years, while jerking off to the ruby red of her lips.

"Where are you going?" I said, standing there like an idiot. *An uninvited idiot. Get out. She's obviously not lying on the floor bleeding.* But I couldn't move. Couldn't stop staring.

That half smile was fucking lethal. "Who says I'm going anywhere?"

"Uh." Good question. It was just that she had changed into fancy underwear and put on makeup, so it seemed like… "What?"

She laughed. "Come here, soldier. I did this for you. Got dressed up for you."

"Oh fuck."

"Do you like it?"

"I'm about to pass out because I forgot how to breathe, so yeah, I like it. But listen…I wanted to tell you, you don't have to do this. Not just what you're wearing but even just having sex. I don't want you to feel like you have to do it to get me to help you." I met her gaze, trying to convey how much I meant this. "I'm gonna help you no matter what."

Her eyes were clear and fathomless, the sapphire of a deep ocean cavern. "I know."

And in that moment, I believed her. She knew I would help her. *She trusted me.*

Then she stood up, and I stopped thinking. My brains shorted out as she swayed over to me in those obscene shoes. My eyes couldn't figure out where to land—the shadowed valley of her cleavage, the taut curve of her belly, the incredible slope of her hips.

She reached up and pulled me down, wrapping her arms around my neck. Her lips found my jaw and sucked on a patch of skin. A rough sound came out of my chest, and my hips jerked. This was moving fast. Too fast.

Alarm bells sounded in the back of my mind. What had changed while I went out for drinks?

Then she was palming my cock through the sweatpants, and I forgot to ask what had changed. Forgot to care about anything but the talented stroke of her hands, the swivel of her hips as she pressed her ass into my palm. *God.*

"You're so beautiful," I said. Inadequate but true.

Her smile was less brilliant this time. "I know."

How many times had some asshole thought she was pretty? More times than I could imagine? So why the fuck was I here? Why had she let me in? That thought wanted to take root, but then she crouched down, taking my pants off as she went. Her fist circled my cock; her mouth sucked me in. My back bowed in response, chest heaving. I groaned as her tongue moved like a goddamn miracle all around the head of my cock. She kept up a steady rhythm that should have had me coming in thirty seconds—but then she pulled back. She edged me until my cock was aching with forced restraint, turned purple and leaking precum in her hand.

"Let me come," I gasped. "Please let me come."

"Selfish," she said like an admonishment. She yanked my balls while I choked out an apology.

"I'll make you come. Please. Let me lick you. I want to—"

"I have a better idea. You trust me, don't you?"

Holy fucking alarm bells. Did I trust her? Sure, I trusted her to say things that were mostly honest, as long as I verified them with my own personal fact-checker. So no…not really. That wasn't trust. That was inappropriate interest. Borderline obsession. Trust would have to be later, when a major criminal player wasn't trying manipulating her.

And now I'd stayed quiet too long.

She went to the dresser drawer and pulled something out. It was long and black and shiny—and for a split second, I thought it was the barrel of a gun. My pulse raced, and it didn't slow when I figured out what she was really holding. A strap on. A rubber cock. I knew exactly what she meant to do with it, and my ass clenched in refusal.

Meanwhile my cock throbbed with desire.

"Wait," I said.

Her smile was lopsided. "Don't have all night, soldier. You want me to put this away, I will."

I didn't want her to put that away, not after I'd seen her. I wanted her to use it on me very much, but it seemed fast. And something about her demeanor was off. This whole setup with the lace and the garter belts. It felt like a seduction, like a trap I should avoid, and I wasn't sure why since we'd already had sex.

Not this kind of sex, though.

"Bend over the bed, Clint," she said so softly I almost didn't hear her. But I saw her lips move, so red and plump I wanted to get down on my knees and worship her. So I did the next best thing and obeyed her.

The bedspread was cool against my chest and against

my cheek. I rested there and clenched my ass together so tight it felt like nothing could breach me. She didn't try to force it in. Not yet. Instead she trailed a finger from my nape all the way down my spine. I shivered as her finger traced lightly over the puckered hole. She ended the caress at the base of my balls.

"I want this to be special for you."

"It's already special," I gasped out.

She proved me wrong. What we'd done before seemed tame now, as I lay there exposed to her. She pressed a kiss to the top of my spine, where her finger had touched. Then her lips traced the path down my back with slow, meandering kisses.

I gasped at the sensation of her lips and tongue on me, of her nipples pressing against my skin. And I knew exactly where she planned to go, because she'd already showed me with her finger.

She kissed down my lower back until she reached my ass. I grew so tense, so *clenched* that she couldn't possibly reach between my ass cheeks—and that was for the best, really. Even though the thought of her mouth on my ass excited me, I didn't want her to do something like that for me.

Didn't want her to debase herself for me.

I would have rimmed her in heartbeat if she'd let me, but she would never have to return the favor.

"Wait," I gasped again, futilely. "Della. Not there. Not-there, not-there," I said, my voice slurring.

"Not where?" She slid her finger between my taut ass

cheeks. Tapped on my asshole. "Here?"

"Please," I murmured, out of my mind. What was I asking for? To get fucked? Not to get fucked? I wanted everything from her, impossible as it was. I wanted both more and less, every single breathless feeling and the sweet nothing-bliss of finding release.

"We're gonna go real easy, okay? Have you done this before?"

I shook my head against the bedspread. "Just…fingers. And thought about it."

"Yeah, I've thought about it too. Never done it. I'm going to go slow, though. Won't hurt you. Okay? And I've gotten fucked in the ass plenty, so I'll be careful with you."

Oh *shit*. The way she said it, like she knew exactly how it felt to get fucked soft—and fucked hard, the kind of ass fucking that tore and injured. "Della."

"Don't make me gag you, soldier. You need another pair of panties to hold between your teeth?"

I groaned, imagining it. It had been so fucking hot to taste her arousal while I'd been fucking her.

She pressed two fingers inside me—fast but careful. I sucked in a breath at the pressure and the cool feel of lube. It warmed up quickly inside me, especially with the friction as she fucked me with those fingers. *Too fast. Something's wrong. Alarm bells.*

Then I heard slick sounds as she must have been lubing up the rubber cock. God, just the thought of her doing that. I couldn't quite see with my face pressed into the bedspread, but the mental image of her stroking her rubber strap-on cock was enough to make me rut against the bed.

"That's right," she murmured. "You fuck that mattress. That's the only thing you're going to fuck tonight."

I had to bite down on my tongue just to stop myself from coming.

Something slick and wide pressed against my asshole. *Her cock.* I shuddered, tensed. Just as quickly, the light pressure was gone. Air swept along my back as she moved away.

"Wait," I begged. "Come back."

I was too far gone to have any pride. Too far gone to be lucid or even conscious. I existed only in the sex-dream world, where my fantasies came true and the witches wore red and black lace.

"Something is missing," she said, her voice muffled. I heard her rummaging through the drawer, and then she was back, her legs between mine, pushing my ankles wider apart. "You're squirming too much. It's not right."

I rocked my hips back, desperate. "Baby. *Fuck.*"

Not coherent. Not making sense. Just strung out on the edge, with my cock rubbing against the wet spot it had made with precum. The drops would have been warm when they leaked out of my cock, but the spot was wet. My dick was burning up, and the contrast threatened to set me off.

Something appeared in my vision. Black leather cuffs with a silver chain. And beside it, a long, thin metal chain. *A spreader bar*, my porn-watching brain supplied. *She wants to use these on me.*

"You ready?" she asked softly.

I was ready to get fucked by her, but tied up? That was different. *Do you trust me?* she had asked, and the answer had been no. Then I remembered James telling me I didn't give a shit about these girls, even when I thought I did. More importantly, I didn't give them myself. Just my apartment or my time. Not myself. Not what Della wanted from me.

It suddenly seemed necessary that I surrender to her, like a gift. The only gift that would mean anything to a woman like this. I'd felt pissed off that she hadn't trusted me enough. Enough to let me help her with Dmitri and whatever else. She'd barely tolerated my fixing her porch step, for Christ's sake. But how could she trust me if I didn't trust her?

I must have been distracted, must have let my guard down without consciously realizing it, because my ass had relaxed. Her mouth was between my ass cheeks, kissing my asshole. I strung up tight, my whole body bending off the bed.

"Jesus, that's so good. So good. More please. More."

She gave it to me, rimming me until I was only babbling sounds of pleasure and grief, so close to coming but not allowed, not allowed. My dick felt raw against the bedspread, as if I were rubbing against sandpaper, but I couldn't stop now. Just humped the bed and groaned and pressed my ass into her face. She wasn't the one degraded here; I was, and I loved it. Oh God, I loved it.

"Cuff me," I managed to say. I felt drunk, drugged, unable to form words, but I said those.

She drew one wrist behind my back and secured the cuff tight. Then the other was attached to it. Bound. Helpless. So fucking turned on. Then my legs got spread even farther apart, my ankles wrapped by more cuffs and held in position by the metal bar. I groaned at the loss of control. *You don't let girls in.* I was letting a girl in now, and the alarm bell was a distant memory.

Then her dick nudged my asshole, and my whole body twitched. I was one big nerve ending, one massive involuntary reaction writhing on the tip of her rubber cock.

Her hands settled on my hips as she pushed the cock inside, inexorably, forcefully. I couldn't help it. I clenched to keep her out, but I wasn't sure she even knew it. The rubber cock just pushed in deeper, splitting me open, making me burn.

I gritted my teeth. "Fuck, that hurts."

"Want me to stop?" She didn't even sound breathless, and I was going to explode.

"I feel you everywhere." It was like she'd invaded my body—not just my ass, but my whole body, filling me up to my fingertips. I pressed my cock against the bed, desperately rubbing. "Hurts. Feels good."

"Guess I'll keep going." I heard the smile in her voice. Then she was fucking me, pulling out and then pushing inside. Each thrust into me felt like the first one, a cold and hot, unforgiving and so damn sweet.

She found a rhythm, and that was the end for me. The friction of rubber against a spot inside me. The steady pulls of the sticky bedspread against my trapped cock.

I yanked my arms against my restraints and tried to drag my legs together, as if that could keep me from coming. But I was held open, helpless to whatever she could do to me, and that was hot enough to make me come all on its own. I shuddered and shouted my release, fucking the mattress just like she'd told me to do.

My mind drifted off into that cloudless night, the space between frantic fucking and cuddling after, the time when you are truly alone and prefer it that way. Then I felt her press a soft kiss to the back of my neck.

That was the only warning I had before a sting replaced the kiss, the sharp pain of a needle followed by the sting as some kind of drug worked its way into my system. I shuddered, barely able to comprehend what was happening, so fast, not right, *alarm bells*, before falling out of the sky. I landed in the water with a crash, losing my breath before sinking under, sucking in water, looking up and asking the moon *why?*

# CHAPTER THIRTEEN
## DELLA

THE THING ABOUT drugs was that they weren't instantaneous. Not like you saw in the movies, where you put a rag over someone's mouth and their eyes rolled back. It took him a while to pass out. But the sedative I injected into Clint still affected him. The small movements he could make, with his hands curled into fists, and his ass in the air, told me that the drug was slowing him down. His speech was slurred too.

"What the fuck?" he said. *What the fug?*

"Della. Why are you doing this?" *Dell… Why're you doooing this?*

It made me sick to hear him ask me that, to know that he was lucid enough to understand what was happening but too drugged to protect himself. My stomach turned over, and I wanted to back down. Could I untie him and pretend this was all some sort of kinky game that had gone wrong?

Then I remembered the fingernails in my garage and forced myself to calm the fuck down.

My sister was sitting in a basement somewhere with her fingernails torn off. She had already been beaten, I knew that, but I'd hoped Dmitri would leave her alone once he'd told me what to do. Apparently I wasn't moving fast enough for him. *Fuck.* He was right to doubt me. I *had* been stalling, but that was over now.

I'd made my choice. It came down to my sister or Clint. It had *always* been down to that, but for a little while, for a blissful few days, I'd pretended I could have both.

The crazy part of all this was that I tried to soothe Clint. I stroked the back of his neck where I'd injected him, trying to ease the pain of entry.

"It'll be okay," I lied. "Just go to sleep. Just rest."

He thrashed in his restraints, wrists pulling against the leather, metal links in the spreader bar clinking. There was no way he could get free, though. He had to have known that, even in his spaced-out state, but he kept trying, kept fighting. It broke my heart, so I stayed there, my head bent next to his, whispering words of nonsense.

"I'm sorry. I didn't want to. I know it doesn't make it okay, but I'm so sorry." I rested my forehead against his shoulder. "I think I fell in love with you. I'm a monster. I shouldn't love you."

But I couldn't let my sister die.

Finally he slumped against the bed with a defeated sigh. I stared at his still body with a growing sense of horror. I had done this. I was *doing* this. And I couldn't even stop yet. I had to deliver his body to Dmitri so I could trade him for Caro.

*Release him. Tuck him into bed. Maybe he won't even*

*remember.*

I was shaking violently. Even when I clenched my hands, my whole arm shook. It came from inside, a chill so strong and so deep that no warmth would reach me ever again.

On my first push, rolling him over, I realized I had underestimated this part of the job. Clint was heavy. Seriously heavy, with long limbs and thick muscles. I had to shove him with all my strength just to get him on his back. His cock was soft now—and still wet from his semen.

Guilt sliced me into a million pieces, not only for doing this, but for doing it during sex. I'd taken something beautiful and made it ugly, but at least I hadn't come. There was no way I could have climaxed, no matter how beautiful he'd looked bound and trusting.

Maybe I could have done it while he was sleeping. Or taken him by surprise in the shower. But there was always the chance he'd overpower me first. And besides, I was used to wielding sex like a weapon.

For a very long time, sex was the only power I had.

I found a washcloth in the bathroom and dampened it with hot water to clean him off. I didn't know why it would matter. Dmitri would most likely torture and kill him, so what did it matter if his dick was clean? If he smelled like sex? But it mattered to me, that small bit of dignity, the pathetic consolation prize of being second place to my sister. So I cleaned him off carefully, gently, and undid the cuffs.

I knew what dignity was worth—worth something,

that was for sure. I knew how being naked could strip you of your dignity. I knew how Dmitri could take advantage. *Dignity.*

Fifteen minutes passed, and I was panting and sweating, but he was dressed now. He wore the same jeans as before and a gray shirt that said ARMY in bold letters. I wasn't sure whether that would be a proper *fuck you* to Dmitri or whether it would feed into his pride. But I figured Clint wouldn't mind. He was a soldier, through and through. This would be his uniform in the least fair fight of his life.

I had found a gun too. It must have been on his person when he undressed. I stuffed that into his duffel bag alongside his clothes and toiletries.

At the last minute, I took the medal out of the bag and hid it in my dresser. If Clint made it through this, I would return it to him—along with the rest of his boxes. If he died, Dmitri didn't deserve this as a trophy.

Then I redid the wrists and ankle cuffs, binding him up again in case he woke up. I left the spreader bar off this time, so his ankles were stuck together. His hands were cuffed in front of him this time, to put less stress on his shoulders. I laughed, a little maniacally. What did it matter, stress on his shoulders?

He would be dead soon.

For good measure I added a blindfold. It seemed like a standard thing to do when kidnapping someone, but I didn't fool myself that there was any criminal logic going on. I just didn't want to see the betrayal in his eyes if he woke up.

It took another fifteen minutes to get him down the stairs without bruising either of us too badly. I ended up more injured than him, having banged my elbow and gone down hard on my knee trying to maneuver him down without us both falling. Over half an hour had passed since I'd first given him the drug, and it made me nervous how long this was taking. I still had an hour's drive, and I wanted to make the exchange before he woke up.

The street was mostly empty. Even the green car I sometimes saw parked a few houses over was missing. I breathed deep in relief and dragged him onto the porch and down the steps that he'd fixed for me. Of course the sturdy new step supported both our weights with ease. Whatever sense of morality I'd had was a fragile thing, made of glass, and now it cut me as it shattered.

I was drenched in sweat and panting by the time I managed to load him into the bed of my trunk. I found the plastic tarp in the garage and used it to cover his body, wrapping it snug around him as if I were tucking him into bed.

Then I went upstairs and got his duffel bag and all his stuff from the bathroom. It would be like he'd never been here at all, as long as I ignored the stack of boxes in my garage. But I'd have to figure those out later.

I tossed it into the back of the truck and pushed the tailgate closed.

"Della?"

I whirled to see Katie standing on her lawn, hugging herself. My heart thudded in my chest. How much had she seen? She said there were only shadows from far away.

"Hi, Katie," I said, giving away how breathless I was.

"Is everything okay?" She stepped forward uncertainly. Her eyes were shielded by large brown sunglasses. They were overkill for the waning afternoon light, but I imagined they were more for hiding her disability than blocking the sun. "Do you need some help?"

My eyes felt wild as I glanced at the huge unmoving lump in my truck bed. Had she seen me load him in there? But no…if a regular person saw their neighbor loading a limp body in their vehicle, they would be way more freaked out. They would probably not even come out and talk to me. They'd call the police, but Katie was just standing there, waiting for me to answer.

"I'm good." I struggled to slow my heart rate and catch my breath. "I'm fine. Just have some errands to run."

She smiled a little. "More errands. You need to relax more."

I managed to laugh a little. "Tell me about it."

"Actually, I was wondering if you could give me a ride."

"Uh…what?" She'd never asked me for that before, and while any other day I would have been happy to help, there was no way I could do it now.

"I need to stop by the pharmacy and pick up these special eye drops." She made an apologetic face. "They've been bothering me all day. I can wait in the car while you do your stuff."

Oh, I could just imagine that: Katie sitting peacefully

in the car while I traded in human flesh with a monster. Yeah, no problem. "I'm sorry, Katie. Really I am. Any other day I would've done it but now... But I'm running late and I have no idea how long it will be. I'll take you tomorrow. Or as soon as I come back. I'm so sorry."

She nodded, as if confirming something. "All right. Well, be careful."

And she stood there waiting—and watching?—as I got in my car and drove away. Her words rang in my ears. *Be careful, be careful.* I might die in that crazy mansion tonight. Dmitri might take it in his head to shoot Clint and me and Caro too, to exterminate us like pests. You couldn't trust assholes like Dmitri, which was why I'd never planned on dealing with them at all.

*God, Caro. Why?* I hated that she'd put me in this position. I hated that she'd put *herself* in this position. Even though I tried not to blame her, it was hard not to think she deserved some of the blame as I drove me and Clint to our deaths.

THE SUN HAD dipped below the trees, casting an eerie yellow glow.

When I turned onto the dirt road leading to Dmitri's house, I found the gate open. *He was expecting me.* He knew I would come. He knew exactly how to manipulate people. Caro was the button he could press and press and press.

I drove through the gate.

The ride was exceedingly bumpy, even in my big

truck, so I had to go slow. Even so, I covered ground more quickly driving than walking, and before I was ready, the mansion was within sight. I parked the truck and got out. Walked straight up to the door without looking into the bed of my truck at all. I didn't want to see him looking back at me, if he had woken up early and if the blindfold jostled aside on the ride over. The chances were slim that would have happened, but I couldn't see the disillusionment in his eyes. By now he knew what I really was.

The door opened before I pressed the doorbell. Dmitri stood there with his greasy smile, the one he thought was smooth and terrifying.

"You made it," he said as if I'd arrived for a party.

"Where's Caro?"

"Watch your tone, darling. And she's inside."

"Well, bring her out. I want to see her. And she better be okay, you dirty fucker." *She better be alive.*

Dmitri smiled pleasantly. "She's very well, actually. You'd be surprised. But I don't think you're in a position to make demands about the order of things. First I'd like to see the package."

"We had a deal," I insisted. I studied the windows all the way to the top, but they were too reflective to see inside and Caro wasn't anywhere. "Let me see her."

"We did have a deal, and I intend to uphold my end of the bargain. You give me what I want, and I won't stop your sister from leaving if she wants to."

I narrowed my eyes. "She's coming with me."

He raised one shoulder in a sort of European shrug.

"That won't be up to me. Assuming you brought me the man."

Every cell in my body screamed to get the hell away from there. Just get in the front seat and drive away with Clint. I wouldn't even take him to my house, where Dmitri would know to look for him now. I wouldn't take him to the police station, where Dmitri had the police chief on payroll. I'd just keep driving forever, through desert and plains. I wouldn't even stop when we hit the ocean. I'd drive on water if it meant he stayed alive.

They say your life flashes before your eyes when you think you're going to die, but it wasn't my life I saw. Not the tiny apartment I shared with my sisters or the dingy club I'd stripped at for years. I saw my future instead. The great expanse of possibility, if things had worked out differently. If Clint and I could have been together. If he had been a regular passenger and I had been a regular girl.

In the end, I didn't have to walk over and see if Clint had stirred, if his blindfold had slipped. Dmitri made that choice instead, striding over to my truck and pulling the plastic tarp out. He stared inside the bed of the truck for a second, and another, and another, and then finally looked at me.

"Is this a joke?" he asked.

"I'm not fucking laughing."

"Neither am I, Della. I want the fucking package. I want that army pig and his *fucking* package. Where is he?"

I stepped closer to the truck and stared into the empty truck bed. "Oh shit."

"Oh shit," he mimicked. "Did you think I wouldn't

notice, you dumb slut? Did you think I would just give you Caro and the two of you would ride off the sunset?"

"No, I—" *Oh God, where did he go? What am I going to do?*

*You're going to die. And it's all you deserve.*

Still, I was trying to figure out where the hell Clint could have gone. I had this horrible vision of him somehow falling out of the truck while we were on the highway and getting crushed. God. *God.* But I would have noticed that, wouldn't I? It seems like I would have noticed his weight lifting from the truck and bouncing out. I would have noticed cars swerving and crashing behind me, even if I'd been in a haze of guilt and self-hatred since leaving my house.

But then I remembered the open gate at the edge of the property and the bumpy road on my way in. I might not have noticed if someone had slipped over the side on a big bump.

*No, that's too much to hope for.*

That would mean Clint actually woke up and managed to get out of the truck while cuffed on his wrists and ankles. It was so freaking unlikely, but my heart already raced with exhilaration. He'd done it. He'd gotten away.

Even the duffel bag was missing, which told me he must have taken it with him. He had his cell phone, his weapon. He'd escaped.

Dmitri grabbed my arms and shook me. "Where is he?"

My eyes scanned the tree line, and without meaning to, I gave it away. Dmitri released me fast enough that I stumbled back. He shielded his eyes from the sunset glare. No movement.

"He's gone," I said, my voice hoarse with relief. "He's far gone by now."

I just prayed that was true.

Dmitri took a phone from his pocket and made a call, snapping in Russian to the guy on the other end of the line. Then he strode over to me, grabbed my arms, and shook me again. My head wobbled on my spine so hard I was dizzy even when he stopped.

"You little stupid whore. I give you one thing to do, and you cannot even finish the job." He ended his little speech by slapping me across the face.

My jaw felt like it unhinged. I shook my head to clear it, ignoring the ache in my cheek. "So maybe you should do your own work instead of blackmailing women to do it for you."

That earned me another brain-jarring slap. This time I lost my balance and fell on the ground. I wanted him to keep going, to keep pummeling me, to give me the pain I deserved for dragging Clint into this mess.

He gripped my chin hard enough that I whimpered. He turned my face so that I had no choice but to look into his pale, haunting eyes.

"You understand you're going to die now," he said calmly.

*I know.* I couldn't speak, my jaw too sore—was it broken?—and his hand clamped it shut anyway. But I told him with my eyes. He'd been crouching over me, leaving himself vulnerable. He didn't expect me to fight back, not when it would lead to more pain for me or for Caro. I was beyond that now. We would both die here, but I wouldn't make it easy for him. I raised my knee and kicked him between the legs.

He doubled over and fell on top of me, pressing us both into the ground. I couldn't breathe. I fought him, struggling to get his weight off me. *I never wanted his weight on me again.* That would be worse than death at this point. I had already resigned myself to dying, but I wouldn't let Dmitri touch me again. Wouldn't let any of those fuckers touch me again. The last man to be inside me was Clint, and I was going to die that way.

Big ideas. I had big ideas, but then Dmitri slammed my skull into the ground. The ground was hard from a recent drought; it rattled my brain and left me dazed. Dazed enough that he could flip me on the ground and put his knee on my back.

He laughed at my predicament. "You've changed since you left."

"I'll take that as a compliment," I mumbled.

"You should. I like a little fight. You and your sister. You always thought I wanted a girl who did what I told them to, but that wasn't it at all. I wanted a girl who fought back. Caro figured that out first."

The weight from his knee increased as he levered himself up. He stood, pressing his heel into my spine until I couldn't hold it in; I sobbed into the dirt, hating that he'd brought me this low again.

He twisted his foot, pressing the hard edge of the heel farther into my spine. "I'll have fun with both of you here."

A crack rang out in the open space, pinging the granite wall behind us. I froze, and Dmitri did too. I angled my head so I could look at the smoking hole where the bullet had gone. Who the hell had fired that? The only ones who'd be here and armed would be Dmitri's men, but why were they shooting at him? Did they mean to shoot me and somehow got it horribly wrong?

I waited for Dmitri to dive for cover. Even he would do so when we were taking fire from an unknown source. He didn't have a death wish.

And for a second it seemed like he had gone for cover as his body landed beside mine and dust rose to cover my eyes and ears and nose. Then everything went silent.

I watched in horror as the dust cleared. Dmitri was lying on his side, his body lax. And his head...God, his head. It had been shot through, that was the only way I could process it. Half of it was missing. I looked at the ground around us and realized it was sprinkled with blood. And hair. *And brain matter.*

I scrambled away, wiping at myself furiously, crying.

Who had shot Dmitri?

Then I saw the figure of a man in the distance, emerging from the tree line. He was tall, with broad shoulders. He walked slowly at first, like someone who had been injured. *Or someone who was cuffed at his ankles.* As I watched, he aimed his gun down between his feet and another crack split the air. Then he crossed the remaining distance quickly.

"Clint," I whispered.

# Chapter Fourteen
## Clint

THERE ARE TIMES in your life when you think you've hit the bottom. Eating MREs and hanging out with international criminals while they brutalize women...that was one of them. That had to be the worst. But then we'd put most of them behind bars. We'd dismantled their organization, and I thought it made things okay.

Then I made it stateside and figured out that my girlfriend was breaking up with me. Worse than that, she'd been cheating on me. Oh, and she kicked me out of my own apartment.

That, I figured, had to be the lowest fucking point.

But I was wrong. Getting *kidnapped* and *almost fucking murdered* by the girl I was seeing. This was the worst.

I figured it out, of course, as I came to in the bumping bed of the truck. I was the payment Dmitri had demanded in exchange for her sister's life. So maybe it should have made me feel better to think she'd tried to offer him money instead, that she'd tried to find some other way.

But I didn't feel good. She'd picked *this* in the end. It hurt bad enough to break me up inside, but I stared at her stonily as I walked closer. I had a lot of experience with this, approaching the enemy.

And as much as I hated to think of her that way, she was the enemy.

Her face was puffy and red from when the bastard had hit her. Those would turn into dark bruises soon. How badly was she injured? Her clothes covered any injuries on her body. She held herself stiffly as I approached. Ridiculous how easy it was to feel sorry for a woman I should hate.

"You okay?" I asked roughly.

I hadn't meant to ask that, but she looked too fucking pitiful, like a dog from the gutter, that I had to throw her a bone. She shrugged, then winced at the movement.

There wasn't much I could do for her here anyway. I went over to Dmitri and found two firearms on his person—tossed them into the cab of the truck.

"Get in," I said.

Della just sat there, her eyes wide, looking past me. *She's going into shock, asshole.*

Yeah, well, maybe she wouldn't be so fucked up right now if she hadn't tried to kill me.

"Get in the truck."

"Can't," she mumbled.

*Shit.* "Something broken? Where does it hurt?"

A humorless smile tilted her lips. "Hurts everywhere, but that's not why. Caro. My sister."

I glanced at the house. "We go in there, we might not come out. There are men patrolling the area. Only a matter of time until they find us."

"You go," she said.

I shook my head. "This is how it's going to happen. You get in the truck, driver's seat. I'll go in and look for her. If I get us out, we all three drive away. If I don't come back, if the guys find you first, then you can assume I didn't find her. Anyone comes here, you drive like a bat out of hell. Got it?"

Her eyes widened. "I'm not leaving you here."

"No, Della. You don't get to call the shots. After what you did, the least you can do is listen to me."

She tried to stand...and stumbled. She finally made it to her feet, swaying in the sunset. "I've spent my whole life doing what men told me to do. Including tying you up and bringing you here, which was the biggest mistake of my life. I'm done with that."

"Yeah, you picked a real inconvenient time to start being independent."

She flinched, and her shame resounded deep in my belly. I knew she deserved my bitterness, my cruelty. And she'd take it all too. I read the guilt in every harsh line of her body. She'd probably let me beat her just like Dmitri had. She'd let me pound her into the ground as if I could take my revenge out on her flesh.

Didn't want to hurt her, though. But I did want to take the revenge out on her flesh in a different way.

*Yeah, you picked a real inconvenient girl to lust after.*

"Take the truck," she said softly. "Keys are in the ignition."

I barked a laugh. "That's not how this works. I'm a soldier in the US Army, do you understand? Do you know what that means to me? It means I have to protect everyone. I don't get to pick and choose."

She shuddered, and I felt her pain roll all the way down her body. It rose to the surface as a deep flush she tried to hide by looking down.

"I'm done arguing, sweetheart. You wanna come get shot to hell? Be my guest. We'll both go in and look for your sister. Just do me one favor. Stay behind me. The last thing I need is you getting us both killed."

Of course it wouldn't happen that way. If anyone was waiting behind a corner ready to spray us with bullets, I would be the first one hit. It wouldn't give Della enough time to get away or defend herself, but it was all I had.

Turned out we didn't have long to test out my theory.

Standing in the middle of the atrium was a blonde woman. Pale blonde hair, creamy skin. A nose that turned up, and a certain bearing. Regal. Elegant. She was shorter than Della, her expression harder, but I could see the family resemblance. And she was holding an automatic pistol with a comfortable grip, pointing directly at us.

Her gaze focused on me. "Arms up. No funny business."

I raised my hands into the air. *No trouble here.* Only took a second to figure out what had happened. We'd gotten played. Della had gotten played.

She stepped forward, a stunned look on her face. "Caro?"

Caro smiled like a hostess would, welcoming but distant. "I wondered when you'd get here."

I took advantage of their conversation, edging farther away. I moved silently—and slowly enough not to be noticed. If I could get a clean shot without attracting her attention, I'd do it. Or if the woman started shooting, I'd draw her fire away from Della so she could escape.

I just had to hope Della took the opportunity when it presented itself. *Get to the truck. Get safe.* I tried to will her the orders, but she was staring at her sister in shock.

Della shook her head, not understanding. Not believing. "What are you doing? You were hurt. I saw the picture."

Her sister smiled indulgently. "You saw what you wanted to see."

"You sent me your...your *nails,*" Della cried, and disgust panged in my gut. This woman was a piece of work. And Della was related to her? No wonder she had a hard time trusting people.

Caro showed us her nails, painted a shiny purple. "You mean these? Pretty, aren't they?"

Piece of work.

Della made a disgusted sound. "You beat up a woman so I'd think you were hurt. And you...you..."

"Tore off her fingernails? Not me personally, but that's the general idea. If it makes you feel any better, the girl was dead by the time that happened. Stone-cold."

Della clapped a hand over her mouth. She got herself under control with visible effort. "No, that *doesn't* make me feel better. You're sick. I can't believe I was worried about you."

"I can. The little martyr girl always running to save me. You kept doing it over and over again when no one asked you to. I knew you'd do it if we *did* ask."

"We?" Della asked.

"Me and Dmitri. Well, I suppose it's just me now. You did kill him out there, right?"

"Yeah." Della's voice was hollow. "I think you're all caught up."

I hated the defeated look on her face. It was worse than her quiet acceptance when I'd walked up to her. I could have killed her then. Someone like Dmitri, the kind of man she was used to, would have done just that. But she hadn't protected herself. She hadn't even cowered. She'd accepted her death as her due, but this was even worse—like she'd just realized she was all alone in the world.

"Took you long enough, little sister. For a second I thought you might not come through."

Della hesitated, looking lost. "I didn't—I couldn't—"

Her gaze flitted to me, and I fell into the broken look in her eyes. I tasted her sadness and breathed in her regret. It didn't matter in that moment that she'd bring Caro's attention to my new position. It didn't matter that we'd both probably die here. All that mattered was that she know I forgave her.

I'd spent most of my life wishing like hell I had a family, wanting one so bad I had to enlist just to make one for myself. Now I had brothers in arms, and I would sacrifice anything to save them. *It's okay,* I tried to tell her without words. *I would have taken a bullet for you. I would have died for you.*

Her expression didn't change, and I had no way of knowing if I got through. But then Caro was there, shouting, "Hey, you, get back over there. What are you trying to do? Hands in the fucking air."

So maybe I'd let them drop a little, as if they were tired, as if they'd sagged naturally. But in reality, I knew it would come down to this. Down to a duel.

Caro raised her gun at me. I watched the angles of our guns shift in slow motion, hers and mine—whoever pointed first, whoever pulled first, would win.

I pulled the trigger and braced myself for the impact of a bullet.

"No, Caro. *No.*" Della's voice sounded agonized, as if she was already mourning one of us. I didn't know which one she meant. *No, Caro, don't shoot him.* Or *No, don't shoot Caro.* But she was closer to Caro than me, since I had been shifting away. She launched herself at her sister, falling short because of a glass-and-gold table in the middle. They fell like dominoes: Della, the table, and Caro last of all.

I watched in shock, in absolute terror, as Della filled the space where her sister had been. "*Della!*"

In those fractured moments, I did something I'd never done before. Not in my foster home when we bowed our heads before dinner. Not in the hellholes overseas.

I prayed.

*Let her be okay. Let her be safe. I'll do anything you want if she's safe.*

I had spent my whole life searching for a place to belong. For a family, for religion. For an army. But I had never felt that deep peace, that all-encompassing comfort, until Della had looked at me and known exactly what I was. She'd known exactly how to deal with me.

She'd given me every damn thing and I couldn't even keep her safe. The fact that she hadn't confided in me, that she'd tried to use me, wasn't an excuse. I should have known. *I should have protected her.*

It felt like digging through the wreckage. There was glass and pieces of a vase and pieces of a table. Water mixed with blood. There was a woman choking on her own breath, dying on the floor. Blonde, slender.

For a heart stopping moment, I grabbed her arm. But as soon as I touched her, I knew. *Not Della.* This was her sister, and Della was already kneeling at her sister's side, pressing a piece of cloth to the wound.

Too late. It was too late to save Della's sister. That was what she'd set out to do, save Caro. But the woman sucking in her last breath on the floor, with her sparkly purple nail polish, had been gone way before now.

# Chapter Fifteen
## Della

I USED TO cry after we went to the strip club. Not just because someone was hurting me or touching me. I would cry all the time. It drove Dmitri crazy. It drove Caro crazy too. I think it reminded her to be sad about what had happened to us. It made it harder for her to move on.

*We just have to play along*, she told me.

For my birthday, she got me a plant. I was so happy. I think I cried again, which pissed her off, but they were happy tears. I thought the plant was like the ones I'd had back at home. I thought it meant she wasn't going to forget, like me. We wouldn't forget.

Then I found out she had done things with Dmitri to get the plant.

I turned the pot upside down over the toilet and let the plant and soil fall in. I flushed it all down the drain and threw the pot away, because I didn't want any part of that. Caro said I was stupid, that I refused to play along, and for a long time, I believed that. Even when I stopped stripping and left Dmitri, I still believed it was stupid. I just knew that if I kept going that way, I would die. I wasn't the scientist in this world; I was the plant, and without enough water or sunlight, I was dying.

That was what I told Clint while we waited for the ambulance to take my sister away. He didn't say anything in return. He just kept his hand on my shoulder. He had done that ever since my sister stopped breathing. He had touched my shoulder or stroked my hair or held my hand, as if he knew I needed that anchor. As if he knew I'd float away without it.

There were a bunch of people in suits milling around outside. Some came inside and started taking pictures. Katie came and stood in front of us. I blinked slowly, not understanding. Katie, my neighbor. *Blink.* Katie was wearing a suit and looking right in my eyes, directly, which she'd never done before.

"Not right now," I heard Clint say, his tone almost vicious. "You can talk to her later."

Katie argued, saying it was important, that things were fresh.

"She's in shock," Clint said. "The last thing she needs is to find out about you."

*I already figured it out,* I wanted to say. I figured everything out, but that didn't seem to matter. Knowing wasn't the problem. Playing along, that was the problem.

The ambulance arrived, but they didn't take Caro. I told them to take her. "She needs help."

But they just shook their heads. Clint steered me out the door, away from Caro's unmoving body, past my neighbor Katie who was no longer blind, and into the back of the ambulance. They stung me a thousand times, finding the places I had been cut and then making them deeper.

"Digging out the glass," they said, but I wasn't sure about that. Couldn't believe what people told you. Couldn't believe pictures of beaten women or real-life nails torn off. Couldn't even believe Clint when he said, "Everything will be fine."

One of the paramedics held up a needle. "This isn't going to hurt."

*Liar.* But I offered him my arm and didn't flinch as it went in. Clint held my hand, murmuring, "I'm here. I'll watch over you. Just relax."

I remembered soothing him while he went under. *Just go to sleep. Just rest.* And I realized that only made it worse. Because in those moments before the drug dragged you down, when the last bit of pain whispered through your body, what you wanted most was not to sleep. I wanted to finally wake up.

# Chapter Sixteen
## Clint

"They're going to give you another medal for this," James said.

I groaned. "Don't even joke about that."

"Who's joking? You did a good thing."

I would definitely not be getting a metal. The only reason they weren't filing charges against either Della or myself was because they didn't want the scandal. Definitely didn't want it getting out that the FBI didn't even *know* about an international crime leader rising in the ranks. It was an embarrassment. Suddenly the damned list was in high demand. At first I thought it had been lost, but then I'd found it in Della's dresser drawer, tucked under the purple and gold medal.

Agent Katherine Porter was thrilled to take it off my hands. She was a hero in the FBI now.

Good for her.

I scrubbed a hand over my face. "All I'm looking forward to is a very quiet, very uneventful rest of my leave."

"I hear that."

Almost getting killed was not a great way to spend my leave. Almost getting Della killed...*fuck*, I still had nightmares. I felt the kick of the gun and saw her body falling, catching the bullet, bleeding. It hadn't happened that way, but my mind was content to replay the horrifying alternate ending on repeat.

I prayed now—not just at night. All the time. But it didn't come out like the words I had read so many times. It ran through my head in a soulful litany: *Della* and *be safe* and *come back to me.* Praying wasn't enough to stop the nightmares. I had even shouted enough at night to scare the nurses. They got a doctor to prescribe me some sleep meds, but then I couldn't sit next to Della while she slept. Then I wouldn't be alert if she woke up and needed me.

I accepted the cup of lukewarm coffee James had bought from the machine. He ordered another drink for himself, something fancier, with chocolate or caramel or some shit. I wanted my coffee black. It was utilitarian, designed to keep me awake with minimal disruptions.

James raised an eyebrow. "Slow down there. What did that drink say about your mama?"

I looked at my cup and saw it was mostly empty. I must have gulped it down. I snorted at his lame joke and tossed the Styrofoam cup across the room. It landed in the trash can. "Three points," I said idly.

I left Della's hospital room several times a day. Or more accurately, I got kicked out several times a day. The doctors and nurses stopped by to check on her or replace stitches or run more tests.

The day after, her face had swollen up and turned

black-and-blue, bad enough to match the picture of that poor girl they'd sent her. But that part would heal on its own. The worst part had come toward the end, when she'd fallen on glass. Some of the shards had cut deep into her hand, piercing tendons and slicing nerves. She'd already had two surgeries to try to repair the damage, and she would probably need physical therapy to regain full motion in that hand.

"What did the doctor say this time?" James asked.

"They're thinking two days now."

He nodded. "Good. Good."

We both knew the psychologist might not sign off on her discharge, though. Because she wasn't talking. Hadn't said a single word since we left Ozerov's country house of mirrors. She wouldn't talk to me or the doctors. Agent Katherine Porter had showed up to take her statement and left empty-handed.

This time they were changing her bedding and bathing her, so I knew it would be a few minutes until they let me back in.

"I'm going downstairs," I told James. "You want anything?"

He shook his head and resettled on the thin plastic chairs that would never be comfortable.

James had been some pretty fucking awesome support throughout this whole thing, and even though I told him repeatedly to go home to Rachel, he told me she wanted him to be right here.

He had been worried when I hadn't contacted him

about searching Ozerov's place. When I didn't answer my phone, he came over to Della's house looking for me. He found Agent Porter going through Della's trash—again. The woman was relentless. And Agent Porter had found the fingernails, so they knew things had gone south. By the time I woke up in Della's truck and called James, they were en route. Too late to save Caro, but no one would be crying over her.

Except Della. Tears fell down her cheeks like rain, one after the other, never ending. I didn't know how her grief could match the skies. I didn't know how to dry up the ocean.

I found myself in the gift shop, which had a lot of cheerful stuff, pink polka-dot balloons and cards that played music and a ceramic figurine of a high-heeled shoe. I thought about getting her something like this— bright and meaningless. But in the end I kept circling the tiny shop, making the clerk nervous, until my gaze landed on a group of little plants in pots.

They weren't flowers. They were some kind of plant with green bulbous ends, flowers made out of cactus pieces. But not sharp. I read the tag. *Succulents.* They were nice, but I liked the one in the back with the green sticks. It reminded me of Della's house, the lush lawn and climbing honeysuckle. So much green. I picked up the pot and wondered if Della would ever speak to me again.

"That's a great choice," the clerk said. At some point she had moved to stand beside me. "The bamboos generate more oxygen than other plants. And they're highly adaptive. They can thrive in most situations, even without fertilizer."

"Oh," I said. I supposed that was good to know, although I'd mostly picked it because it looked pretty and earthy and elegant—like Della.

"It's actually a type of grass," the clerk continued. "With very strong stems."

I raised my eyebrows. "You gotta learn all this to work here?"

She flushed. "No, but I'm a biochem major."

"Good for you," I said, and meant it.

"Did my junior thesis on these things. Anyway, do you want it? It'll be $14.99."

I sighed, wishing there was something bigger and nicer and more expensive. Of course I wished for that. I was always trying to give money, according to James. A bleeding heart. A fucking martyr. I shook my head, disgusted with myself.

But this was somehow worse, because I didn't want to give her my money to help her. Didn't want to give her a plant because she needed or wanted it.

I had to give her something, to stay by her side, to keep trying to talk with her—for myself. I wasn't a martyr with her. No, my motives were purely selfish. I needed her to talk to me so I could hear her voice. I needed her to look at me so I could watch her expressive eyes, sweet and so alive. I needed her to forgive me, forgive herself, so that I'd have a chance at a real future with a woman I shouldn't have fallen for. But I had, all the same.

# CHAPTER SEVENTEEN
## DELLA

I DRIFTED IN a dreamworld, never sure which people were real. The doctors, they were real. And the nurses. They would push needles into me, and seconds later, minutes later, I'd feel a faint sting. Even pain didn't wake me up.

Caro wasn't real, though. She came sometimes, standing by the door, holding her finger to her lips. *Shhh.* She was protecting me, then. Other times her face contorted in rage as she reached for me with purple claws. But neither of them were real, because Caro was dead. I'd watched her die. I'd held her limp hand and found no pulse.

James. That was his name. Clint's friend. I wasn't sure if he was real. I watched without curiosity as he came in after the nurse left.

He sat down in the chair beside the hospital bed. "You don't mind if I wait with you, do you? Clint's going to be back any second."

I said nothing, just watched him.

He closed his eyes with an expression of bliss. "God, an actual cushion. It's like a miracle. Do you think Clint would notice if I switched this with one of the chairs in the waiting room?"

Funny. *Smile.* There was a time I would have smiled in reaction, but I'd forgotten how to do that. The muscles on my face were still asleep. The parts of me that could laugh or feel happy were still asleep. This whole thing might have been a dream.

James studied me. "Clint's worried about you. I'm guessing you know that. I'm also guessing you're doing the best you can, but if you can give him any reassurance…" He shrugged. "He just wants to know you're okay."

I thought about that. Was I okay? I was dry and warm. I had a bed that wasn't exactly comfortable but it would do. No one was hurting me, except the doctors and nurses sometimes. Yeah, I was okay.

There was a sound at the door, and Clint appeared. A dream? Real? Everything just felt so far away. But maybe the world was actually fine. Maybe I was the one who had left.

Clint looked good. There were shadows under his eyes, probably because he hadn't been sleeping well. Hard to sleep in a plastic chair, even one with a cushion, with his head propped up in his hand. He'd been there every time I woke up from a nightmare, shushing me, telling me it would be okay, and I'd thought he was part of the dream.

It was easier to think he was part of the dream than to face him. Face myself. Face what I had done.

I had gotten my sister killed.

I had almost gotten myself killed.

I had almost gotten Clint killed.

Clint, who kept ordering food from the cafeteria and putting it in front of me, as if I'd suddenly discover a deep-seated desire to eat Jell-O and dry toast. *Eat just a little*, he would say. *Have a bite.*

And I would stare at him, wondering why he didn't hate me. He didn't hate me, so he must be a dream.

Now Clint was holding something. Not food this time. Not coffee. A bamboo plant. It was small and green, in a square pot glazed in a white and blue china pattern. I flashed back to a different time, a different plant, and my heart started to pound. *What bad things did he have to do to get that plant?* I was stuck in the in-between space, neither past nor present, but mired in my fear of the future.

He held up the plant as if for inspection. "I thought you might like this. Thought it might make the room a little..." He waved a hand toward the gray hospital room, looking uncertain. Was he nervous? "Brighter."

Looking at the plant made a strange feeling well inside me, like liquid pooling in the center of my chest, pressing down on all my vital organs, crushing them. So I looked at the sheets instead. At my hands, twisted together.

"It's a...uh, bamboo. For luck. That's what the tag says. And the lady at the store..."

I stared at him like he'd lost his mind. *Luck?* He

wanted to give me luck? I was the opposite of luck. I was basically the grim reaper in a flight attendant uniform. I was…getting a little dramatic, even in my own mind.

"Why are you here?" My voice came out hoarse and rusty.

His whole body tensed at the sound, as if he had to restrain himself against doing something big and possibly violent. Grabbing me? Holding me? I wanted him to hold me. But he got himself under control. When he spoke, it was with a wariness that broke my heart.

"I got you this plant," he said.

"I don't want your plant."

"Okay," he said easily and reached his hand out to toss it in the trash. *Throwing it in the trash. Flushing it down the toilet.*

"Wait!"

He stopped and watched me like *I* was the crazy one. And okay, fair point. But I wasn't actually crazy. I was just tired. I was dreaming. I was waiting to wake up.

Clint set the plant down on the cabinet that held the monitor. *Beep, beep, beep.* Still alive and breathing. He sat in the chair James had vacated, wincing as it creaked under his weight. He was a big guy. The chairs here couldn't hold him. I couldn't imagine him fitting in the hospital bed I was currently living in. But for all his innate power, he looked almost hopeless. Like he didn't know what to do.

*He just wants to know you're okay.*

Was that why he kept coming back? And if I told him

I was okay, would he stop coming? The thought filled me with cold dread. I'd never see him again, but it wasn't fair to bind him to me, anchored by his fierce need to protect.

"I'm feeling a little better," I offered.

Something flashed through his eyes, swift and blinding. He spoke mildly, still careful. Still cautious. "You had me worried."

"I'm sorry I didn't talk because…" I wasn't really sure how to explain it. "I guess I didn't know what to say."

For three whole days.

He reached out a hand and then pulled it back. "It's okay not to talk. You were attacked and brutalized. It's okay to be afraid, and I didn't want to push you too fast. But I don't even know if you want me to stay or…"

"Stay." Regret panged in my chest. "Or don't. I wouldn't hold it against you. I mean…I tried to kill you. I think breaking up with me is kind of par for the course."

His lips twitched. "Were we dating?"

For some reason, a flush spread up through my chest and heated my cheeks. "Maybe not in the traditional sense."

The look in his eyes told me he remembered in exactly what *sense* we did connect. Hot nights beneath the cool sheets. Kissing feverishly in the kitchen. Bending him over the bed and pegging him…right up until I'd betrayed him.

"No," he agreed. "Not in the traditional sense. But in a way I'd like to try again. Without the…you know…"

I remained silent, wanting to see how he'd describe it.

"Without the psychopathic maniac pulling your strings," he said.

My eyebrows shot up. Pretty good description, actually. The only thing I didn't like was that it removed the responsibility from me. "I don't understand why you're even talking to me when I tried to kill you. I should be in jail."

He shrugged even though I could tell he was uncomfortable. "He played you. You don't need to feel bad about that. He played a lot of high-ranking law-enforcement officers too."

"And Caro?" I asked softly.

"Her too. Her most of all. She was the reason they were after that list." When I raised my eyebrows in question, he nodded. "Ozerov's name had been on the FBI's radar for a long time. I had even heard about him overseas. The problem with guys like that is getting enough evidence to convict."

"But my sister wasn't on any watch lists."

"That's right, which meant she could travel without anyone questioning her. She went to Russia, to China. She dealt directly with the manufacturers and made herself important in Ozerov's organization."

"But why?" I asked, bewildered. She could have gotten away. We both could have gotten away.

Clint's eyes were sympathetic but implacable. He wouldn't let me escape the truth about my sister, not anymore. "Money? Power? Why does anyone become a murderer?"

I flinched. In my case, I knew exactly why, but it didn't relieve me of my responsibility.

"Not you, Della. You're not a murderer. You didn't want to hurt me. You think I don't know that? I figured that out in the bed of your truck, while we were bouncing along at ten miles per hour. I figured that out when you were holding me, crying, after you'd stuck me with that needle."

My eyes were wide. He was yelling now, and it was like a cold splash of water on my face, yanking me out of sleep. This was what I'd been looking for. His anger. His disgust. I didn't deserve his sympathy—didn't deserve him at all.

He stood and paced the floor. He ran a hand over his hair and then turned to face me. "Of course you'd protect your sister. And of course I'd help you. Yes, even if I died to do it. You think I'd go to another country and die for a stranger, but I wouldn't die for you? I'm yours, Della. I've been yours since you first offered me some goddamn peanuts on the flight home."

I stared at him, unable to speak, but for a totally different reason this time. There were too many things I wanted to say. Questions I needed to ask. I had to ask whether he meant it when he said he was mine. My heart beat too fast and my breath came too short to form any words. It didn't matter, because he wasn't finished.

"God, Della. I wasn't mad that you turned me over to Dmitri. I was mad that you didn't trust me enough to tell me the truth. I could have told you he wouldn't hand your sister over if she was really a hostage. I could have helped you plan the exchange to stay safe. Or at least, given you my gun and taught you how to use it. You almost got yourself killed, and *that's* why I'm fucking pissed."

My chest felt tight, the air in my lungs growing, expanding. "Oh," I managed.

"Yes, *oh*. And what I really want, if you're looking for some way to make things up to me, is to get out of this damned hospital and never come back. I want to be barefoot in your kitchen frying bacon. I want to be bent over your bed, getting my ass reamed and—"

A small sound came from the door. We both looked over at James, who was standing there holding a cardboard container of two coffees and a bag from the café downstairs. His mouth was hanging open. He looked scandalized.

"I'll just...leave these here." He deposited the food and drinks on the nearest flat surface and bolted from the room.

"Well, shit," Clint said in the following silence.

The strange airy feeling inside me popped, like a balloon, and a small laugh huffed out of me. That turned into a giggle. Clint gave me a repressive look, but then his lips quirked. Then he was laughing too, a big laugh with his hands on his knees. Laughing woke me up like nothing else could have done. Laughing did what pain and sleep and guilt could never do. Laughing brought me back.

# Chapter Eighteen
## Clint

I WAITED FOR what felt like hours, straining to hear anything coming from outside the room. Logically I knew only a few minutes had passed, but every second beneath the blindfold expanded in time, like a drop of water in a well.

My hands were free. I could just rip off the blindfold. My ankles were unbound. I could leave this room, find Della, and push her up against a wall. But the anticipation made the edge of arousal sharper.

My cock was tenting the front of my cargo pants. My faded army t-shirt, usually so freaking comfortable, felt like sandpaper against my nipples. *Find her. Take her.* But she had promised the wait would be worth it...

A sound came from the door. I tensed as I heard Della's familiar footsteps enter the room. How many times had I heard her enter, waiting with my face pressed against the headboard or pushed into the mattress. I had come to know Della well in the past few weeks, but she had come to know me even better. She knew how to make me squirm. How to make me beg. How to make me hurt so fucking good I couldn't wait to do it again.

"Patience," she said, correctly reading the frustration in my body.

I tried to relax. And failed.

There was something different today, a change in the cadence of her walk. My mind scanned through possibilities like the whirring of a slot machine. *Cha-ching.* She was wearing shoes on the carpet. I hoped they were her black stilettos. She wore them and pressed them to my skin, and I practically came on contact.

A whisper of air beside me carried her scent. There she was, so close. Then her hands were light on the back of my head, tugging the fabric, loosening the blindfold until it fell in my lap. I stared in shock at the sight that greeted me. In the upstairs bedroom of Della's white house, she was wearing her blue stewardess uniform. Her hair was pulled into a tight bun. Her makeup was crisp, lips a deep ruby red. I let my gaze fall down over her slender hips and long legs. God, those legs. All the way to her shoes. Not black stilettoes. These were navy blue to match her uniform, shiny patent leather, shorter and more practical to walk in but no less sexy. More sexy, because they were part of her prim-and-proper uniform. She'd worn it just for me.

"Della," I said hoarsely. I had to cram so much into that word. *You're so beautiful. I'm head over heels for you. I love you.* Things I couldn't say when she was looking at me like she wanted to eat me up.

She glanced down at her name tag. *DELLA,* it said in bold capital letters. "That's right." She smiled. "Can I get you something? Water? A soda?"

I swallowed, remembering those questions on a plane three weeks ago. My mouth was impossibly dry, desperate for something to drink. "No, thanks," I said.

I didn't want a soda. I wanted to lick the moisture from her skin, and from the look in her eyes, she had a plan to get us there. She smiled again. "I think I can rustle up some pretzels if you ask nicely."

The way she said *pretzels,* I knew she wasn't talking about food. She was talking about tying me up in knots, and it was too late, really. She'd made knots inside my body—around my heart and up to my brain. Tied in a bow around my cock. Invisible ropes that never chafed; they just reminded me who I belonged to. They would stay even when I was deployed again. Even when she was on a plane. Even when I sat in a chair in her bedroom and pretended to be a passenger.

"I'm not very hungry," I said. "But there is something you can help me with."

Her eyes sparked with pleasure. "Oh, what's that? I do aim to please."

I suppressed a groan. The woman pushed all my buttons—every single one that made my body turn into flames. "The problem is I can't get this seat belt working."

We both looked at my lap, which of course had no seat belt whatsoever. My cock, however, thought this was a great time to pulse and leak precum into the army-green fabric of my pants.

"I'm so glad you told me about that, sir. I have just

the thing to help hold you down... In the event of an emergency, of course."

"Of course," I murmured in agreement. My breath hitched as she pulled out a wide black strap. It was made of a stretching material, designed for multiple uses. For tying wrists together or attaching large, willing men to antique headboards. It did look remarkably like a seat belt as she draped it over my lap and pulled it tight. Much tighter than a seat belt would normally go, but the restraint just made my dick throb.

"Oh no," she said. "This won't do. You aren't safe at all like this."

"What's wrong?" I asked, sounding worried, playing along. "Can you fix it?"

Her voice was directly behind my ear, low and breathy. "I'm going to fix you right up. Just hold very still."

I almost laughed at her playful seduction, but I was too busy trying not to come. It took all my concentration to hold back when she bound my arms beside my body— for my safety, of course. Then she realized that my feet were in danger as well. They needed to be secured to the legs of the chair.

"Unfortunately the windows must stay open for the convenience of your fellow passengers," she said sadly, holding up the blindfold. "You'll need this if you plan on resting at all."

My eyes were covered, and then she was kneeling in front of me. "Della, please. Please."

"What's this?" The lightest touch stroked along the bulge in my pants. "A wet spot here. Did you spill your drink?"

I groaned again, my breath coming more shallow. "I don't know."

"No, you won't be comfortable that way. Here, let me wipe that up for you." Her finger circled the tip of my cock, spreading the precum all around, pressing more of it into the fabric.

She made a dismayed sound. "Oh no, it's getting worse. You'll catch a chill, all wet like this."

As if to prove her point, I shuddered and bucked my hips against her hand, my cock desperate for more contact. Desperate for her.

Thank God she was never cruel. She knew how much I needed her in that moment, and she opened my pants and took out my cock. I panted as she stroked me once, twice.

"This is the problem." Her voice was authoritative now. A bit relieved, since she'd found the origin of all that wetness. "See, here? You're leaking."

Her finger swirled around the tip of my cock, and I choked out words I couldn't even recognize. "Baby. Help me."

"I'm going to help you, sir. That's my job. But you'll need to call me Della. Professionalism is vital on the job."

"Yes, Della," I gasped.

"Good. Now I'm going to do my level best to clean up all this wetness. And you're going to be a very good boy for me and stay quiet, aren't you? You don't want to disturb the other passengers."

The sound I made was a cross between a grunt and a whimper. Then her tongue touched the tip of my cock, and I moaned long and low. "Della," I muttered, in agony, having to stay quiet instead of shout my ecstasy.

"Shhh," she said. "I'm just cleaning up this mess. Look how much of it you have. And even when I lick some up, more comes out of the tip. What are we going to do about that?"

She licked me, over and over, while my thighs shook and my abs quivered. I was rocking my hips in the chair, threatening to break it apart. Then her mouth encompassed me, all the way down to the base, and I couldn't hold back anymore. I was bursting, I was broken in pieces, but I forced myself to stay quiet while I shattered.

"Della. Oh, *Della.* I'm coming, baby," I whispered as I pumped come into her mouth.

She cleaned me up with long licks that turned into leisurely pumps. I didn't know how much time passed on that chair, in that blindfold, but my soft dick turned hard again. She licked and sucked and bit my chest until I was begging her to let me go, to touch her. I wanted to eat her out, but when my dick was hard enough, she climbed on top of my lap and impaled herself on my cock.

I shuddered at the feel of her swollen flesh.

She sighed in clear pleasure. "I used my mouth on you. I sucked your dick, sweetie. Didn't I?"

"Oh, Jesus. Yes. So good."

"Then why don't you return the favor, hmm? Use your mouth on my breasts. Suck them."

*Thank fuck.* I'd never touched her breasts before now. Never licked or sucked or bit them. Because she'd never ordered me to. But now I was released, and I tasted her soft flesh and sucked her tight nipples.

Her muscles tightened around my dick, and I groaned. Then her pace sped up and I couldn't hold on to her breasts without hurting her. I kissed her neck and buried my face in her hair as she rocked her hips on top of me. Faster and harder, she slammed herself down on me until she shuddered and moaned and clenched around my dick with enough force to milk me all over again.

When our breathing slowed, she got up and took me out of the restraints. She tried to massage my arms, to make sure I was okay, but I wouldn't let her. Her hand wasn't fully healed yet, and damned if I was going to risk her comfort or her health so that I could get a rubdown.

In bed, I pulled her close, tucking her head under my chin and holding her tight against my body. I loved being dominated by her during sex, watching that sexy body move, doing whatever wicked thing she wanted me to. But I also liked to protect her.

I wanted her to feel safe next to me, her smaller body against my larger one, her sweeter nature against the hard-hearted training of a soldier. I knew she thought of herself as a cold person, a cruel one, but I'd never met anyone who met my needs before her. I'd never met anyone who gave me her house, her body. Her hopes for the future.

There was no woman more kind and generous than her, and I counted myself lucky to be the one to serve her.

"You okay?" I asked with a contented sigh.

"Never better." Her voice was thick with sleep. "Thank you for asking."

I smiled, feeling my eyelids shut. The world narrowed to her and me. "Anytime, Della."

"And thank you for flying."

# THANK YOU!

Thank you for reading *On the Way Home*!

I hope you loved Della and Clint's story as much as I do…

If you enjoyed this, you'll love the sexy, gritty Chicago Underground series! Book one *Rough* is available as a free download from all retailers.

I'm a cautionary tale. A statistic. A victim. A single teenage mother from the poor part of town. Most of the time I'm too busy working and struggling to care what people think. Survival doesn't come easy.

I have a dark secret, a pressure valve, a rare moment just for myself. On these nights I visit a club. There I find men who give me what I need.

Men like Colin.

But he wants more than a few stolen hours. He demands more than my body. He wants my heart and soul—my happily ever after. I never thought I'd be Cinderella. I never thought a man that rough could be my prince.

> "This is a book you MUST read if you like gritty, edgier romance that makes you think as well as turns you on."

Sign up for my newsletter at skyewarren.com to find out when I have new books!

You can also join my Facebook group, Skye Warren's Dark Room, to discuss Hold You Against Me, the Stripped series, and my other books.

I appreciate your help in spreading the word, including telling a friend. Reviews help readers find books! Please leave a review on your favorite book site.

Turn the page for an excerpt from Rough...

# EXCERPT FROM ROUGH

THERE'S A CERTAIN sultry walk a woman has when she's bare that can't be faked. No hose and no panties. The nakedness under my skirt was as much about keeping me aroused as it was about easy access.

I'd perfected the art of fuck-me clothes. A surprising number of men asked me out, even at a grungy club on a Saturday night. Cute little college girl, they thought, out for a good time. I saved us all time by dressing my part.

Tonight's ensemble consisted of a tight halter and short skirt with cheap, high-heeled sandals, bouncing hair, and bloodred toenails. The scornful looks of the other women didn't escape me, but I wasn't so different from them. I wanted to be desired, held, touched. The groping fingers might be a cheap imitation of intimacy, its patina cracked with rust and likely to turn my skin green, but they were all I deserved.

My gaze panned to the man at the bar, the one I'd been watching all night. He nursed a beer, his profile harsh against the fluid backdrop of writhing bodies. His gray T-shirt hung loose on his abs but snug around thick arms, covering part of his tattoo.

Dark eyes tracked me the way mine tracked him.

His expression was unreadable, but I knew what he wanted. What else was there?

He was hot in a scary way, and that was perfect. Not that I was discerning. I needed sex, not a life partner. There were plenty of men here, men whose blackened pasts matched my own, who'd give it to me hard.

A woman approached him. Something dark and decidedly feminine roiled up inside me.

She was gorgeous. If he wanted to score, he probably couldn't do better, even with me.

I tried not to stare. She walked away a minute later—rejected. I felt unaccountably smug. Which was stupid, since I didn't have him either. Maybe no one had a chance with this guy. I was pretty enough, in a girl-next-door kind of way. Common, though, underneath my slutty trappings—brown hair and brown eyes were standard issue around here.

"Hey, beautiful."

I glanced up to see a cute guy wearing a sharp dress shirt checking me out. Probably an investment banker or something upstanding like that. Grinning and hopeful. Had I ever been that young? No, I was probably younger. At nineteen I had seen it all. The world had already crumbled around me and been rebuilt, brick by brick.

"Sorry, man," I said. "Keep moving."

"Aww, not even one dance?"

His puppy-dog eyes cajoled a smile from me. How nice it might feel to be one of the girls with nothing to worry about except whether this guy would call tomorrow morning. But I was too broken for his easy smile. I'd only end up hurting him.

"I *am* sorry," I said, wistfulness seeping into my voice. "You'll thank me later."

Regret panged in my chest as the crowd sucked him back in, but I'd done the right thing. Even if he were only interested in a one-night hookup, my type of sex was too toxic for the likes of him.

I turned back to the guy at the bar. He caught my eye, looking—if possible—surlier. Cold and mean. Perfect. I wouldn't taint him, and he could give me what I craved. Since Tall, Dark, and Stoic hadn't deigned to make a move on me, I would do the pursuing. A surprising little twist for the night, but I could go with it.

I squeezed in beside him at the bar. Up close his size was impressive and a little intimidating, but that only strengthened my resolve. He could give me what I needed.

"Hey, tough guy," I shouted over the din.

He looked up at me from his beer. I faltered a bit at the total lack of emotion in his face and fought an automatic instinct to retreat. His eyes were a deep brown, almost pretty, but remote and flat. Dark hair was cut short, bristly. His nose was prominent and slightly crooked, like it had been broken. Maybe more than once.

He looked mean, which was a good thing, but I was used to a little more effort. Even assholes provided a fake smile or smarmy line for the sake of the pickup. There was a script to these things, but he wasn't playing his part.

My club persona and beer from earlier lent me confidence. Whatever was bothering him—a bad day at the construction site or maybe a fight with the old lady—I didn't care. He was here, so he needed this as much as I did.

I planted my elbow on the bar. "I saw you looking at me earlier."

He raised an eyebrow. I shrugged. He was making me work for it, but I found myself more amused than annoyed.

"Buy me a drink?" I asked.

He considered me, then nodded and signaled the bartender.

The beat of the club reverberated as I took a sip. "So do you talk?"

His lips twitched. "Yeah, I talk."

"Okay." I leaned in close to hear him better. "What do you talk about?"

He ignored my question—or maybe answered it—by asking, "What are you doing here?" Almost like he was asking something deeper, but that had to be the alcohol talking.

"I'm trying to get laid, that's what I'm doing here." I pulled off a breathy laugh I was pretty proud of.

He didn't react, didn't appear surprised or even interested, the bastard. He just looked at me. "Why?"

I decided on honesty. "Because I need it."

He seemed to weigh the truth of my words, then nodded toward the exit. "All right, let's go." He got up and threw some cash on the bar.

His easy acceptance caught me off guard, just for a moment. But it shouldn't have surprised me, be-cause...well, because men always wanted sex. That's what I liked about them—they didn't even bother trying to hide it. It was worse when I hadn't seen it coming, when it had sneaked up on me—Now wasn't the time to think of that. It was never the right time to think of that.

He tucked his hand under my elbow, guiding me. He used his body to maneuver us through the crowd, almost as a shield. The whole thing was so gentlemanly, given what we were about to do, that I wondered if he'd heard me right. Maybe he'd want to get coffee or something, and wouldn't that be awkward all around?

But he was a man, and I was a woman wearing fuck-me clothes—this could only end one way.

When we exited the club, I couldn't help sucking in several deep breaths. Even the faint smell of street sewage was refreshing, washing the stench of smoke, alcohol, and countless perfumes from my lungs. I never liked the crowds. The press of bodies, the mingling smell of sweat, the small bumps from all around. Tiny violations that were somehow okay since everyone did it.

As my heart rate settled, he inspected me as if he could read me. He couldn't. "What's your name?" I asked to distract him.

"Colin. Yours?"

"Allie."

"Nice to meet you, Allie. Your place or mine?"

I was comfortable again. I knew this play: horny girl who can't wait to get naked.

"We don't need to go anywhere. Let's get started right here." I let a soft moan escape me and clasped myself to the brick wall named Colin. Never mind that I was dry as a bone. He wouldn't notice. They never did.

He raised his eyebrows. "In the parking lot?"

"Or in my car. Whatever. I just want you to do me."

"I'm not fucking you in a car. It's forty degrees out."

I was hardly in this for comfort. I'd done it in colder weather just this past winter. "I don't mind."

"Well, I do."

"Fine." I was willing to give him so much. Why couldn't he take it the way I wanted? "Then we can go to the motel over there. You're paying."

He didn't look happy. I wasn't either, but I couldn't budge on this. Going to an apartment might be the norm for hookups, but my hookups weren't normal.

Going to their houses where they might do God knows what was out of the question. And I wasn't about to bring one of these guys home.

"Not there," he said. "I'll pick the place."

✧ ✧ ✧

I FOLLOWED HIS truck in my car to a motel about ten minutes away. When I pulled in, he waved me to a parking spot next to his truck and went into the office.

The place wasn't fancy, but the manicured shrubbery and freshly painted building proclaimed this was an entirely different kind of establishment than the dump by the club. No renting rooms by the hour here.

The sign out front advertised $119.99 a night. A typical price for Chicago, but I sweated the cost. The extravagance of my six-dollar drink from earlier paled in comparison.

What if it was too much money? I might not be worth it.

I kept watch on the frosted office door like he might disappear. Eight minutes later, he came out. My stomach clenched. He flashed a key and nodded toward the back before getting into his truck. I followed him in my car and pulled up beside him again.

It was dark back here. Deserted. The only light came from flickering, yellow lamps dimmed by tiny hordes of bugs. Scattered buildings slumbered around us like a nest of dragons, their snore the low drone from the appliances. It wasn't exactly safe. Technically that was what I wanted, but the allure of danger only worked up to a point.

He didn't come to my car. Instead he opened the motel room door and waited.

I could drive away. He probably wouldn't even come after me. Even if he could, if I drove somewhere safe—assuming there was such a place—there'd be nothing he could do.

But his solemn patience gave me the courage to open the car door and join him.

The stale air and harsh edge of cleaning supplies softened me. I'd ridden along with my dad in his 18-wheeler once. He usually slept in truck stops, but with me he'd gotten motel rooms. This was just an empty room, but it felt strange to use a place for casual sex that I associated with childhood memories.

Once inside the room, I set down my purse on the floral fabric chair.

Colin reached out and trailed his finger along my jaw. His eyes, almost black in the dark motel room, searched my own. I thought he was going to fuck me then, but he said, "I'm going to make coffee."

I blinked. Shit, coffee. "Okay."

He went to work at the coffeemaker. Unsure of what to do, I sat down in the chair, clutching my purse in my lap like I was waiting for a doctor's appointment instead of rough, dirty sex.

He poured a cup of coffee, adding the cream and sugar without comment, and handed it to me. I took a few sips. It soothed some of the skittishness I hadn't realized I had. He didn't take any for himself.

*Enough of this.*

I set down the cup on the cracked countertop and stood to kiss him. I started off light, teasing, hoping to inflame him. This was all calculated, a game of risk and power.

He kissed me back softly, gently, like he didn't know we'd started playing. He held his body still, but his mouth roamed over mine, skimming and tasting.

It wasn't a magical kiss. Angels didn't sing, and nothing caught fire. But he wasn't too rough or too wet or too anything, and for me it was perfection.

I rubbed against him, undulating to a rhythm born of practice. His hands came up, one to cup my face, the other around my body.

I sighed.

He walked me backward, and we made out against the round fake-wood table, his hands running over my sides, my back. Avoiding the good parts like we were two horny teenagers in our parents' basements, new to this. I shuddered at the thought. This was all wrong. His hands were too light. I was half under him already, my hips cradling his, so I surged up and nipped at his lip. Predictably his body jerked, and he thrust his hips down onto me.

*Yes. That's what I need.* I softened my body, surrendering to him.

"Bed," he murmured against my lips.

We stripped at the same time, both eager. I wanted to see his body, to witness what he offered me, but it was dark in the room. Then he kissed me back onto the bed, and there was no more time to wonder. The cheap bedspread was rough and cool against my skin. His hands stroked over my breasts and then played gently with my nipples.

My body responded, turning liquid, but something was wrong.

I'd had this problem before. Not everyone wanted to play rough, but I was surprised that I'd misread him. His muscles were hard, the pads of his fingers were calloused.

I didn't know how he could touch me so softly. Everything about him screamed that he could hurt me, so why didn't he?

I wanted him to have his nasty way with me, but every sweet caress destroyed the illusion. My fantasy was to let him do whatever he wanted with me, but not this.

"Harder," I said. "I need it harder."

Instead his hands gentled. The one that had been holding my breast traced the curve around and under.

I groaned in frustration. "What's wrong?"

He reached down, still breathing heavily, and pressed a finger lightly to my cunt, then stroked upward through the moisture. I gasped, rocking my hips to follow his finger.

"You like this," he said.

Yes, I liked it. I was undeniably aroused but too aware. I needed the emptiness of being taken. "I like it better rough."

Colin frowned. My eyes widened at the ferocity of his expression.

In one smooth motion he flipped me onto my stomach. I lost my breath from the surprise and impact. His left hand slid under my body between my legs and cupped me. His right hand fisted in my hair, pulling my head back. His erection throbbed beside my ass in promise. I wanted to beg him to fuck me, but all I could do was gasp. He didn't need to be told, though, and ground against me, using my hair as a handle.

That small pain on my scalp was perfection, sharp

and sweet. Numbness spread through me, as did relief.

The pain dimmed. My arousal did too, but that was okay. I was only vaguely aware of him continuing to work my body from behind.

I went somewhere else in my mind. I'd stay that way all night.

At least that's what usually happened. Not this time. Instead I felt light strokes on my hair, my arms, my back. His cock pulsed hot against my thigh, but he didn't try to put it inside me, not in any of the places it would almost fit. His hands on me didn't even feel sexual. He petted me, and I arched into his caress.

*Want to read more? Find Rough on Amazon.com, BarnesAndNoble.com, iBooks, Kobo, and Google Play!*

# Other Books
# by Skye Warren

*Standalone Dark Romance*
Wanderlust
On the Way Home
His for Christmas
Hear Me
Take the Heat

*Stripped series*
Tough Love (free prequel)
Love the Way You Lie
Better When It Hurts
Even Better
Pretty When You Cry
Caught for Christmas
Hold You Against Me

*Chicago Underground series*
Rough
Hard
Fierce
Wild

Dirty

Secret

Sweet

Deep

*Criminals and Captives series*
Prisoner

*Dark Nights series*
Keep Me Safe

Trust in Me

Don't Let Go

*The Beauty series*
Beauty Touched the Beast

Beneath the Beauty

Broken Beauty

Beauty Becomes You

The Beauty Series Compilation

Loving the Beauty: A Beauty Epilogue

# About the Author

Skye Warren is the New York Times and USA Today Bestselling author of dark romance. Her books are raw, sexual and perversely romantic.

Sign up for Skye's newsletter:
www.skyewarren.com/newsletter

Like Skye Warren on Facebook:
facebook.com/skyewarren

Join Skye Warren's Dark Room reader group:
skyewarren.com/darkroom

Follow Skye Warren on Twitter:
twitter.com/skye_warren

Visit Skye's website for her current booklist:
www.skyewarren.com

# COPYRIGHT

This is a work of fiction. Any resemblance to actual persons, living or dead, business establishments, events or locales is entirely coincidental. All rights reserved. Except for use in a review, the reproduction or use of this work in any part is forbidden without the express written permission of the author.

On the Way Home © 2014 by Skye Warren
Print Edition

Cover design by Book Beautiful
Formatting by BB eBooks

Made in the USA
Middletown, DE
19 June 2016